GRAIL QUEST

THE SHADOW
COMPANION

Read all of the Grail Quest Books!

GRAIL QUEST

THE SHADOW COMPANION

LAURA ANNE GILMAN

HARPERCOLLINS*PUBLISHERS*
A PARACHUTE PRESS BOOK

Grail Quest: The Shadow Companion
Copyright © 2006 Parachute Publishing, L.L.C.
Cover Copyright © 2006 Parachute Publishing, L.L.C.
Cover art © Don Seegmiller

Library of Congress Catalog Card Number: 2006017719

ISBN-10: 0-06-077285-9 (trade bdg.) — ISBN-13: 978-0-06-077285-7 (trade bdg.)
ISBN-10: 0-06-077286-7 (lib. bdg.) — ISBN-13: 978-0-06-077286-4 (lib. bdg.)

1 2 3 4 5 6 7 8 9 10

First Edition

For Ty Wheeler:
honorary nephew,
natural troublemaker

PROLOGUE

The great Merlin, court magician to Arthur, High King of Britain, and the most powerful enchanter in the known world, was on the verge of losing his patience.

This wasn't an entirely unusual occurrence: In fact, most of humanity made Merlin lose his temper on a regular basis. But he had expected better of Ailis, the young maid who had recently shown herself to be a magic user of no small talent.

"Girl-child," Merlin began again in a voice he clearly thought was kind, even fatherly. But all it did was make Ailis angrier.

"I'm not a child, Merlin. I haven't been a child in a very long time." There might have been room to argue that a year ago when she was merely one of many servants in Camelot. But not now; not after she and the squire Gerard and the stable boy, Newt, had rescued Arthur and his court from Morgain's sleep-spell; not after she herself had been taken prisoner by Morgain; and not after she had discovered that the sorceress was plotting even more wickedness against her half brother, the king.

And not now, since she had been sent, with Gerard and Newt, to accompany the chosen Knights of the Round Table on their search for the mystical, magical Grail Cup—the holy relic that Arthur could use to solidify his hold over his kingdom. This relic, according to Merlin, was their best hope to keep Morgain's plots at bay.

"No, you're not," Merlin agreed, running one hand distractedly through his hair, the shoulder-length strands flying wildly. "And that is exactly why it is so important that you do as I say."

She was ready to protest again when Merlin held up one hand, palm outward. "Ailis, do you understand, truly understand, the importance of this Quest?" He didn't wait for her to answer, but went on. "You can *not* imperil it. To be blunt, you—and I and everyone else—are not as important as finding the Grail. Specifically, finding the Grail before Morgain does."

"Is it really magic?" Ailis asked. Morgain had insisted that, whatever the Grail's origins, the fact that it was a blood-blessed chalice made it part of the Old Ways more than the new, and therefore hers by right, more so than Arthur's. Ailis had never considered that before, but it made sense when Morgain said it. Then again, many impossible things made sense when Morgain said them. That was half her charm, and most of her danger.

"Magic?" Merlin shrugged, his old, worn robe shifting around his body like a living thing. "Anything people don't understand, they call magic and blame it or worship it or—I am more concerned with what I know it is: dangerous."

Ailis's confusion showed on her face, so he sighed and tried to explain again. "The Grail is power, Ailis. No matter what it may *actually* contain within it, people *believe* that it is the cup which held the Christ's blood, and that makes it a symbol of leadership, of authority."

"That's why Arthur wants it."

"That is why *I* want Arthur to have it. Arthur desires it because he, too, believes." Merlin's voice held a resigned fondness, as though he had argued the point with his king many times before. "Morgain wants it because if Arthur had it, he would have an authority she lacks and cannot make up in any other way."

Ailis wasn't sure she understood, but Merlin went on before she could ask him more questions. "But the real danger, Ailis, the real danger lies not with the Grail, or in which leader has it. The danger lies within the Quest itself. . . ."

He stopped then and looked at her. Clearly, he was waiting for her to work it out for herself.

Thinking out loud, she did so. "Whoever gains the Grail, whoever finds it and returns it to Arthur . . . that knight will have much glory." But she knew that wasn't it, not alone. Glory would not concern Merlin. "Glory . . . and influence. He would be seen as pure enough to have won the Grail, pure enough to be without sin . . . and Arthur, so enchanted by the legend of this Grail, would be swayed by the word of a knight such as that. Perhaps too much."

The enchanter's approving nod was enough to make Ailis flush with satisfaction, offsetting the unease she felt about speaking so bluntly—and unflatteringly—about her king.

"So you understand?" he said. "The Quest must continue. For it to fail would play into Morgain's hands. The Grail must be found, or at least kept from Morgain's grasp. It must be done in Arthur's name, without hope of personal gain. Only then can Arthur's throne be secure—and Camelot be safe, forevermore. The Quest *must* succeed."

Ailis sighed, unable to argue with the passion in Merlin's voice, and returned to the original point of their conversation. "So I'm to use no magic at all? Not even to help us accomplish our goal?"

"You need to keep practicing, of course. And yes, as needed . . . but, chi—Ailis, do nothing that will draw attention to yourself or distract the knights from their Quest. Troublesome or not, they are the ones who must find it, not Morgain's forces."

"Merlin, I'm the only female on the entire Quest. You are aware of that, aren't you? Half the knights keep trying to help me across mud puddles, while the others treat me as though I were something—" She stopped herself mid-speech, and ended instead with "something that has no business being anywhere near this oh-so-holy and noble pursuit of theirs—as if I haven't already proven myself, and far more often than many of them!"

In fact, no matter what Merlin said, Ailis wasn't confident that the knights on this Quest had any chance of success. The Grail was a holy relic no matter which god you chose to follow, and only one of pure spirit and intent should find it. Ailis believed that with all her heart. Unfortunately, since the Quest had begun, what she had seen from the flower of knighthood was closer to pigs shoving over bits in the trough than men of valor and glory. Maybe if Lancelot were here, or Gawain . . . But they had instead gone with Arthur, dealing with the uprising of a northern border lord who challenged Arthur's right to the throne. Then they had each gone off on their own to seek the Grail, rather than trying to catch up with the other knights. She suspected they would have more luck individually than with all the knights of Camelot put together, anyway. And Merlin could stop worrying, because neither Gawain nor Lancelot would ever do anything to harm Arthur, intentionally or not.

Ailis pulled at her braid and stared at the enchanter. With his sharp black eyes, he was much better suited for staring than Ailis could ever manage—and she blinked first.

Normally, Ailis trusted Merlin implicitly. He was much older and wiser, if occasionally a little scattered and distracted by his magical nature. But when it came to being female, she sometimes wished she were back with Morgain. The sorceress might lead the opposing side against Arthur, Ailis's sworn and chosen king, but she was another female, and at least she understood.

Ailis turned and strode away from the enchanter, her feet kicking up dust from the ground underfoot. Her shoes were tough, practical things, and she liked the way they hit the dirt when she stomped back to him.

"Ailis. You're wasting energy."

"What does it matter?" She glared at him, angry again. "It's not as though you want me to use that energy for anything else. In fact, you want me to pretend I'm not even here—be a meek, good little mouse so nobody will be made uncomfortable by my existence."

The enchanter's robes drifted in a subtle breeze, but he was otherwise untouched by the dust of the field Ailis was standing in. Which was reasonable, as they didn't actually exist where he was. The two of them were communicating through the astral plane, the magical layer of existence just above the physical world. The only reason he could see her surroundings was because she was re-creating them magically.

In fact, Merlin was several days travel to the south, back in Camelot, in a civilized place where people behaved in a civilized manner . . . mostly.

"Merlin, if I don't practice, I'll go mad. There's nothing else for me to do! You *know* these knights and their squires. You know how they are!"

"Rude, suspicious, arrogant, and quarrelsome. And those are the well-behaved ones. Yes, I know. Ailis, that is another reason why it's important you not do anything to rouse their suspicions. For me, they know I'm Arthur's man. I've pledged myself to him, foreswearing any other loyalties under pain of damnation. That makes me, if not safe, then at least a known threat. You're a young female, and to them that says—"

"Morgain."

"Yes. Morgain." Or Nimue, Merlin's last student, who had—in a fit of pique—locked him in a magical house made of ice before Morgain had first attacked with her sleep-spell. Ailis was female and magical, and therefore potentially dangerous in a way these men didn't quite understand. To them, females were chatelaines—housekeepers—or servants, or wives, or off under the tutelage of religious orders. Women were not sent on great adventures, wearing leggings under their skirts for easier riding, staying in the company of men rather than other females, riding about the countryside. And they certainly did not carry within them the power of magic.

"You sent me here," she said softly. Merlin had to dip his head to hear her, even though magically he could simply have amplified her voice to be as loud as he needed it. "You sent me—us—on this Quest. Why, if not to help?"

"You will help, Ailis. You will, in fact, be essential. I just don't remember how . . . yet."

Part of the enchanter's magical heritage was that he lived backward in time, getting younger as he aged, remembering things that had not yet happened, but not knowing which actions would set them in motion. There were rumors that he was insane. In truth, he was just always confused.

"I need you there, so when the time comes, you'll be ready. And that means not having annoyed any- one so that they won't listen to you when it is time.

"Continue to practice. But stay low. Be well-spoken, gentle, demure." He smiled at her then, the rare mischievous spark reappearing in his eyes. "I know it's difficult, but they're not all that smart, most of them. A little effort, and you can have them all eating out of your hand like pet ponies."

There was a noise behind him, some sort of distraction. "I must go. Girl-child, be careful. Be discreet. That's all we're asking of you." He was clearly speaking for Arthur's wishes now, as well.

She nodded grudgingly, feeling as though *she* were a pony being lashed to harness against her will.

Merlin looked relieved, then focused his gaze intensely at her, his hawk-like eyes now worried in an entirely different way.

"I wish . . ."

She waited.

"You will be all right? With . . . other things? Not the knights, but . . ."

She was the one who smiled then, her face lighting up with bittersweet affection for her reluctant teacher, who was so clearly uncomfortable with what he was trying to say. *Poor Merlin.* He was so very, very bad at relationships himself, the idea of him giving advice . . .

"You mean with Gerard and Newt?" Ailis suppressed a sigh. That was an entirely different kind of stress; one she would have to work out for herself, somehow. "We'll be all right. We won't let you down."

Not entirely reassured, Merlin merely raised a

hand in farewell and turned away, stepping out of the shared astral space. He disappeared back into Camelot's reality with a whirl of his formal gray robes and red slippers.

Despite herself, Ailis had to smile again. Merlin was unique. He was also right: She had to be more patient. She just wasn't very good at it.

ONE

"You have the manners of a crow and the voice of a cockerel, wrapped in the body of a mewling coward."

"And you, sir, are white-necked, flower-hearted, and weak-kneed."

The two men glared at each other, hovering near their swords.

"Hold!" A strong, masculine voice rang out under the arched stone roof, echoing impressively.

Sir Matthias was older than many of the knights on the Quest, but he had a pair of lungs that had lost nothing over the years, and he knew how to project his deep voice over an entire battlefield. Filling the hall of a relatively small monastery was no difficulty at all. Even the carvings of saints in niches on the wall seemed to stiffen and stand a little straighter at

Matthias's bellow. The two knights who had been exchanging insults did likewise, but did not back down completely.

Soon after leaving Camelot, it had become evident that the group of forty-seven knights and squires was simply too large to move smoothly on such a far-ranging quest. Squabbles had broken out over whose tent was placed where, or whose squire did which group chores. Within days, factions began to form within the band of knights—even among those who should have known better.

Sir Matthias, whom Arthur had assigned to oversee the Quest, came to a rapid decision: to break the Quest down into four smaller, more mobile groups, and send each off in a different direction, under a trusted and sensible lieutenant.

He thought that would make the knights in each group focus on what they were meant to be doing. It hadn't quite worked that way.

Sir William glared at Sir Bart. The gaggle of monks backed away from the two men, looking to Sir Matthias for help in keeping violence out of their sacred halls.

"Take it outside!" he ordered his knights, then turned to make an apology to the abbot without waiting to see if his command was obeyed.

"We gave you hospitality for the nature of your Quest," the religious man said, his cowl pushed back as he spoke to Sir Matthias. "And this is how you repay it, by bringing discord into a house of the Lord?"

The rumor that the Grail had once rested in the stone chapel of this monastery on the fog-shrouded coastline had brought Sir Matthias's group westward. But there—as in so many places before—the rumor had faded into ancient mist. The monks did have a story of a man dressed in strange clothing, who had come to the chapel when it was new-built. He stayed the night. But other than a shred of white fabric that might once have been an Apostle's robe—or the hem of some kitchen maid's apron—they had nothing to show for it.

The disappointment had pushed several of the knights into squabbling about their worthiness, suggesting that various sins—real or imagined—were the reason why their group had not yet discovered any trace of the Grail's whereabouts. It was at this point that Sir Matthias had stepped in.

"I apologize, good Father. We shall remove ourselves at once, and leave you to your prayers and contemplations."

The abbot looked sternly at Sir Matthias. "You are men of sword and blood, seeking a thing beyond your ken. Not even the High King has the right of ownership of the Grail. It is a thing of faith, of a greater glory than that of this mortal world. Remember that, and perhaps your own faith will be rewarded."

Gerard, standing at Matthias's left side, had a fleeting thought that he would like to set this abbot against Merlin when the enchanter was at his most obtuse, and see who cried for mercy first. He kept that thought to himself, however. Newt and Ailis would have appreciated it. But Newt and Ailis were not with him.

The abbot left the hallway, and Sir Matthias indicated to his men that they, too, should depart. As they walked through the great stone doors of the monastery, Sir Matthias gazed up at the pale blue autumn sky and shook his head.

"Sir?" Gerard stood by the knight, looking into the sky for whatever had caught the older man's attention. A midday storm would delay their departure and make the men even more unhappy, but it certainly wasn't cause enough to make Sir Matthias appear that troubled.

"Nothing, lad. Nothing. Come, I'll need you to help me prepare."

That was Gerard's job on this Quest. Since his master, Sir Rheynold, was not on the journey, he had been assigned to Sir Matthias by the king himself. He was to be a sort of aide to him, assisting in the running and organizing of the Quest.

Gerard had assumed at first that the new title was just a fancy, courtesy term for squire, and that he would, in fact, be shining armor and cleaning boots, among other familiar chores. But Sir Matthias had a squire already who did those things, a young boy named Jon, who was bright and eager and very green.

Instead, once Sir Matthias discovered Gerard could write, he found himself oft as not with quill in hand, taking notes while the knight paced and spoke, or carrying highly sensitive messages to and from the other knights, or—as was the case this day with the abbot—asking to arrange a meeting.

In the weeks since the Quest had ridden out of Camelot, Gerard thought that he had learned more of how to manage men than he had in all his years with Sir Rheynold. Not to dismiss his master's talents, but Sir Matthias was a leader, rather than a warrior.

His way involved not the swing of a sword, or even the rallying of men to his side, but the more subtle coaxing and chivvying of men to propel them the way he wanted them to go.

And, when that failed, he had a strong sword-arm as well.

The walk back to the encampment was a quiet one. The first thing a squire learned was to speak only when there was need, and to never, ever interrupt a knight while he was thinking. Sir Matthias was clearly thinking, and thinking hard.

"The trouble is," the gray-haired knight said finally, as they were climbing the last yards of rock-lined path to the meadow where their encampment had been settled, "the trouble is that our Quest, our journey, is too vague. 'Find the Grail,' we were told. As though the very virtue of our noses might direct us to it. It led the men to believe that the task would be simple, as though they were on one of the queen's May Day jaunts to fetch flowers, not a long-lost holy artifact!"

Gerard hesitated, his need to show himself worldly warring with his promise not to divulge any-thing of what Merlin had said before sending the three young friends to join the Quest. The desire to impress Sir Matthias won. "Merlin said that magic might be—"

Sir Matthias rested a heavy hand on Gerard's shoulder, cutting off his words. "I will speak no word against Merlin, who has proven himself in service to our king. But magic has no place on a Holy Quest. It profanes the search, and I am ever thankful that Arthur understood this and did not allow his enchanter to interfere in our search."

Gerard wasn't sure Merlin could have done anything that directly, even if he were asked. He had seen enough to know that magic, while fabulous and a little frightening, also had limits. If Merlin *could* whistle up the Grail, Arthur would already know of its location. Suddenly, Gerard wondered how much of Arthur's original dream of the Grail and his decision to send knights in search of it was of his own inspiration—and how much was he influenced by advice from Merlin.

"I don't know how he does it, Gerard," the knight said. "I don't know how the king keeps us all in line."

They passed by a number of other pavilions. Squires were seated outside working on equipment, walking horses to the stream, or running various errands, waiting for new orders. In the distance, toward the center of the encampment, four or five of the twelve knights Sir Matthias had kept with him were gathered in a tight knot, clearly focused on something on the ground.

That sight did not improve Sir Matthias's mood at all. As they reached the larger tent which served as his home and headquarters, Sir Matthias shook his head, this time in resignation.

"Either gambling with dice or fighting. I have a desire to take them all out and horsewhip them, save it would do no good but make them surly."

"Sir, if I may be so bold . . ."

"Go ahead," Matthias said, lifting the door-flap of the simple canvas pavilion. He gestured for Gerard to go before him.

"Is it always like this? When they're not being watched, is it always thus?"

As he entered, Gerard saw Ailis out of the corner of his eye. She was seated on rugs piled four deep, putting something away. Her expression was one of deep thought and mild discontent.

At the very beginning of the Quest, Sir Matthias had taken one look at her—Ailis being much the same age as his own daughter back home—and had insisted that she sleep in a corner of his tent, for propriety's sake.

Ailis hadn't done anything other than curtsey and say "thank you," but Gerard got the feeling she wasn't happy staying here. He didn't understand it— he'd gladly have traded the discomfort of sleeping on roots and dirt for one of those rugs underneath him at night and a roof, however simple, to keep out the rain. Hadn't the three friends complained of exactly those things during their mad rush to find Morgain the first time? They still rode together most days, when Sir Matthias didn't require him, and Newt wasn't helping out the various pack animals elsewhere. . . .

"No," the knight said, distracting Gerard from his thoughts. Sir Matthias unbuckled his sword belt and dropped it carelessly on his cot for his squire to put away. One did not carry a blade into a monastery—not without extreme cause—and so he had left his great sword in the wooden stand inside the pavilion by his bed. From there it could be taken up at a moment's notice, even if Matthias was just waking from a deep sleep. "No, it's not always like this. When men have purpose, when they have a direction, they are magnificent creatures.

"You know this from your own adventures. The sense of life that fills you, the surge of inevitability, knowing that the day can only end one way."

Ailis was shamelessly eavesdropping now, her expression less gloomy. Her hair was braided and pinned up on her head. Gerard missed the sight of her red plait swinging freely over her shoulder, the way she wore it back in Camelot when they were younger.

Sir Matthias saw Gerard watching Ailis and moved his body between the two, an obvious move to break Gerard's study of his friend. Despite his growing fondness for the girl, Sir Matthias had clearly decided that any deepening of the relationship between Gerard and Ailis would be unsuitable.

The knight went on with his commentary as though nothing had happened. "But for now, chasing after this dream of ours, we are lacking that surge, that sense. And so men find other things to do with their energy. And that will include bragging and brawling, if I do not give them direction. Lord, to think that this is the best of Camelot!"

He pulled off his formal surcoat and replaced it with a more comfortable, worn one. To this he added a simple belt, and an ivory-handled knife in an unmarked leather sheath. "I must go speak to two particular troublemakers now, to make sure they do no further damage to each other. Do not hold up the evening meal for me."

With a nod to Ailis, he walked out, sure that his unspoken reminder to Gerard—that he was not to spend too much time with the girl—was understood.

Gerard understood. But despite his respect for Sir Matthias, it went unheeded.

"You think he will succeed?" he asked Ailis, referring to both the two troublemakers and the Quest in general.

"Not without a horsewhip," she said grimly. He stared at her, but she merely went back to whatever she had been doing over in her corner. She pulled a small wooden box the size of her palm out of her pack, slipped her shoes back onto her stockinged feet, and followed Sir Matthias's path toward the doorway.

"Where are you going?"

"Must I account for my every movement to you?"

Gerard was taken aback by the sharpness in her voice. He knew that Ailis had a temper, but it seemed extreme in response to a simple question. He had never thought that she would be the one to heed Sir Matthias's objections, and turn away from *him*.

She saw his confusion, and her face softened. "I'm sorry. It's . . . female things," she said, and lifted the box as though that would explain everything. Suddenly Gerard didn't want to know. Female things were not anything a squire needed to know about.

Ailis left the pavilion with an air of relief. The more time Gerard spent with Sir Matthias the more like the knight he became. While there was nothing wrong with Sir Matthias—she certainly preferred him to Sir Daffyd, who stank of stale herbs, or Sir Ballin, a man who never missed a chance to make a comment about the "inferiors" on the Quest—she missed the old, less self-conscious, less officious Gerard. The Gerard who had once waded into a creek to battle a bridge troll only to require rescuing himself, and was even able to laugh about it afterward. Knowing that things had changed for all of them didn't make the results any easier to bear.

From the way the two of them had been talking when they came in, she assumed that discussions with the monks had not gone well. She could have told them that the night they arrived. The stone walls of the monastery were fine, indeed quality work that would doubtless stand a hundred or more years, but there was no feel of magic to them; no sense of the awe or wonder that Morgain said permeated any area where a magical object had spent any length of time.

The Grail was magical, even if it was not magic itself. Too many people believed in it for it not to be magical. Faith was power.

Ailis believed that magic was power. Not physical strength, but the ability to do, to create. She once shared these thoughts with Gerard. She told him that the Grail is supposed to embody power—the ability to create a High King. She said, "So that's magic. Because the source of magic is belief. You know it exists, the way you know the wind and rain are real. And so you trust in that belief. Merlin said that. You have to believe."

"The Grail is more than magic," Gerard had retorted. "It's faith. Something you don't know and can't prove. You simply have to . . . have faith."

Faith might not be magic, but Ailis knew enough now to understand that belief was essential to both. And if you did not believe, you did not succeed.

As she walked, her feet pressed down on grass that hadn't been trampled by male feet. She followed a trail that led into a narrow copse of trees. Sunlight barely reached through the branches. For a moment, she was plunged into dusk, until the narrow path carried her to a smaller meadow on the other side.

The grass was almost knee-high here, and scattered with small yellow thistles and white bindweed. The smell of dirt and fresh air was a welcomed change from the musty, musky smell of leather and metal that filled the camp.

Satisfied that she was alone, Ailis bent down and placed the wooden box she had brought with her on the ground. She opened it up and withdrew a long, knotted piece of string.

It was a simple spell, one of the first Morgain had taught her. Merlin had said she was to practice. And she *was* far away from anyone who might notice. All the knights were being scolded by Sir Matthias, and the squires would be taking advantage of the free time to do . . . whatever it was boys did when their masters were busy.

She wasn't doing anything wrong. You never knew when you might need to raise the wind—to move sails along or distract the nose of a predator.

Holding the string in both hands, she ran the fingers of her left hand up and down the knots, her lips moving in a soundless invocation.

Once . . . twice . . . the third time she repeated it, her voice was barely audible. The wind in the trees behind her rose in volume. A fourth time, and clouds began to shift across the sky. Her hand stilled on the string. There was no need to go all the way to gale force. She had told Merlin she would behave, and not draw attention to herself. Creating a storm out of nothing was not, by anyone's rules, being proper or demure.

"Nice breeze."

She dropped the string, and the wind died. "Newt."

"I was taking a walk. I saw you and decided to follow." He circled around so that they were facing each other. He had gotten taller since they left Camelot. She used to be able to look him directly in the eye. Now she had to tilt her head up slightly. Upon examination, Ailis decided that he still needed to do something with his hair other than brush it with a piece of straw when he woke up.

As though of its own accord, her hand reached out and smoothed down his rumpled black hair, trying helplessly to get it to lay flat. His hair was rougher than Gerard's. She had known Gerard many years; they had been children together, running through the halls of Camelot on the sort of errands they sent pages and girls on.

But Newt, for all that they had been on such adventures together, was still an unknown to her. He could be so stubborn, so dismissive of everything he didn't approve of—like magic—and yet he was courageous, too, when he needed to be. He had even braved Morgain's castle, despite hating magic the way he did, to rescue her.

She hadn't actually needed rescuing, but that was beside the point.

Newt made her feel so uncertain, always wondering what he was thinking, what he was going to do. With Gerard, she knew. Newt was . . . different.

"You didn't think maybe I wanted to be alone?"

"I think maybe you're alone too much."

"What is that supposed to mean?"

He gave a huge sigh. "I don't know. But you were all alone in Morgain's castle—yes, I know she was there, but she left you alone a lot—you said so. And now you're here, and it's not like you have anything to do, and I thought—"

"Do me a favor, all right? Don't think. You're not designed for it." Her words were sharp, but his accusation had gotten to her. She *was* alone. She *was*

27

useless. And she didn't need a stable boy's concern for her to make it even more obvious.

"Fine, then. I'll go."

"Yes. Do that."

The moment he was gone, she wanted to call him back. She felt sorry for snapping at two friends in such close succession. Instead, she picked up the string, and started whispering the spell again.

*   *   *

"Magic. It makes you mad." That was the only explanation Newt could conjure for the way Ailis was behaving. She had spent many days with Morgain, and with Merlin. It was driving her mad, the same way they said it had driven Nimue mad, which she must be, to play such games with Merlin and distract him from what he needed to be doing.

A sense of unease moved through Newt whenever magic came into play. It shifted under his skin, raising the hair on the back of his neck and the tops of his arms. Magic. He didn't trust it; didn't like it. Never had.

He felt sorry for Ailis, and would keep his promise to Merlin to watch her and make sure that the hooks Morgain had set into her mind and soul didn't do any further damage.

But if she didn't want him around, he wasn't going to lurk in the grass like some lovelorn courtier trying to get a glimpse of his lady-love. As the sole stable boy brought along on the Quest, he had responsibilities beyond keeping one female out of trouble.

Newt liked the feeling of being responsible. In the stable at Camelot he was one of the youngest to care for the horses, having only recently been moved up from minding the dog kennel. And on their journeys, he had been mostly deadweight. Useful occasionally, but not in charge. Never in charge. It was always Gerard's skills in battle or Ailis's magic that saved the day. Knights *needed* him, even if it was only to ensure that their mounts were all healthy and well cared for, and the mules content enough to carry their burdens. It was simple work, and not as time-consuming as being back in the stables. He was learning a great deal by observing the actual conditions his charges were put through daily.

Unlike Ailis, he knew where his place was, and he was satisfied.

Having abandoned the girl to her sulking, Newt walked back out into the sunshine and was immediately engulfed in the calls of several squires who wanted to know where to water their horses now that several of the other squires had foolishly fouled the small inlet in the creek they had been using.

Yes. The things he knew—the homely, ordinary things he knew—were needed. *He* was needed.

TWO

"Witch-child, where are you? I can feel you, I can sense you, but I cannot see you. Who is hiding you from me? Is it Merlin? Never fear, I will find you."

The scrying crystal shimmered slightly in response to Morgain's words, but the haze did not clear. Whoever was protecting the girl from her—and she could only assume it was Merlin—was doing an excellent job of it.

"Arrrgh!"

Her hand swiped over the crystal and it shimmered again, then shattered in a silent explosion, disappearing as it broke apart. A waste, but she felt better for the momentary release of frustration.

A cool hand rested briefly on her bare shoulder, and she pulled the fur robe up more securely, brushing off the contact. She wanted no comfort, not from that hand. Although the workroom was perfectly insulated and heated, she felt a shiver in her bones; a shiver she refused to let show.

"Let go of the girl, my lady. There are more important things which require your attention at this moment."

The voice was as cool as the hand, but Morgain had spent her entire life listening to what others were *not* saying as much as what they were, and she heard the disdain in those tones. Looking over her shoulder, smoothing her plush red, fox fur robe with one hand, she merely raised an eyebrow at the speaker, half daring more to be said.

The shadow-figure was dressed today not in its usual flowing robes and billowy hood, but dark leathers more suitable for travel, with a woolen cowl that came up over its shoulders and covered the back of its head. Even when looking closely, its features were obscured from view, as though the moment a person tried to see its face, their vision would fail.

"Your goal is within sight, Morgain. You must concentrate on that. Let go of the girl. She will still be there when this is done."

The sorceress rose from her chair and made her

way to a map on the wall. Small, glowing lights moved over the outline of an island, and in the waters just off the coastline. Pale blue, cold white, and dark red—each color indicated different factions. Blue for Arthur's forces, white for Morgain's. Her allies were smaller in number, but more cunningly placed, hidden in the common farms and towns throughout the land. Arthur might have mighty warriors, but she would have the element of surprise. The red dots, the allies her companion promised would rise to her aid, were invisible to all who might seek to discover them.

"I am thinking beyond . . . to the next day's goals," Morgain said. "And I'm looking to the months and years after that. Do you have the supplies you requested?"

The shadow-figure nodded in assent: A shipment from the Isle of Apples, Morgain's magical stronghold, had arrived that morning.

"Then go work with them. When the next gift for my brother is ready, inform me."

One delicate hand traced the cold lights on the map. Then she pulled a canvas cover over the entire map, hiding it from sight. The word "gift" was ironic—it will not be given to him; it will not give him satisfaction or pleasure. But one could gift another with frustration as easily as joy.

She noted that the shadow-figure was still hovering nearby. She commanded, "Go!"

The ghostly creature went, with irritation clear in every line of its body.

Morgain sat back down at her worktable and called a new crystal out of storage. But she did not immediately use it.

She needed her companion's aid and assistance. There was no way, humbling and hateful though it was to admit, that she could have gotten this far on her own, not with the level of coordination her plan required. But soon, when the time was right, when the stars were ready and the gods appeased, she would be in position to strike. One blow, sharp and hard and fast, and the island would belong to the people again. *Her* people, not the Romanized fools that ran it now, cut themselves off from the very spirit of the land.

Who did they think caused the grains to grow, the people to increase in number, the winds to rise properly for ships to reach these shores? It was not man, with his sword and shield. It was not man, with his armor and horse.

She snorted, an unkind noise. It was not man who had first tamed horses, either. But they forgot that. They forgot everything.

She would be the one to remind them.

And for that, for now, she needed her companion. But not forever.

*   *   *

"Where have you been?"

"Nowhere."

"Nowhere?" Gerard repeated the word with disbelief. Sir Matthias hadn't returned yet from his meeting with the knights, and Ailis had been gone just as long. It was already well past dusk and raining steadily. He had been sitting on the edge of Sir Matthias's cot, sharpening the edge of his own dagger. His blade was a simple one, but it required as much care as Sir Matthias's more elaborate, expensive one. Ailis's return was a welcomed break from the monotony of stroke and test, stroke and test, but he couldn't imagine what had kept her out so long, especially once the weather began to worsen.

Ailis let the pavilion's flap fall down again behind her. "Gerard, leave me be. I'm neither your sister nor your wife, and you have no right to order me about." Her tone was as mild as she could make it, but warning signs were clearly placed. He ignored them, his concern overriding common sense.

"Ailis, I—the storm. Is that your doing?"

Hours ago, clouds had begun rolling down from the north. Sir Matthias had ordered everyone to move their gear under cover. The rain had started coming down soon after that, and was now pelting hard on the pavilion's roof as though trying to imitate the onset of Noah's flood. The grass outside was now slick with mud. Throughout the encampment, men and dogs remained under cover, while horses nickered and flicked sodden tails patiently.

Inside, Matthias's tent was warm and dry, with expensive beeswax candles giving the space a soothing golden glow that was at odds with the gloom outside. Sir Matthias was many things, but miserly was not one of them, and he did not begrudge spending money on his people, either.

"I don't know what you're talking about." Ailis took off her heavy shoes and outer jacket, shaking as much water as she could off her skirt and blouse before giving up and sitting down cross-legged on the pile of carpets with a sodden lack of grace.

She was nowhere near as wet as she should have

been, considering the downpour, but Gerard refrained from pointing that out. He merely handed her a cloth, and sat back to watch while she unbraided her plait and rubbed her hair dry.

"Magic, Ailis. I'm talking about magic. Storms like this don't simply blow in out of clear blue skies. They have to be called." Although to be fair, it was autumn when rain was more the norm than not. Starting the Quest now, rather than during the originally planned and much drier summer, was purely due to the delays caused by Morgain's mischief. Still, if she had not meddled, he would not be on the Quest at all. Thoughts like that, curling around and chasing their own tails, made his head hurt.

"Because you know so almighty much about magic?" Her scorn was thick and understandable. "And did I use magic to make the monks decide not to help us? Or cause the knights to squabble? Oh, did I also use magic to make the laundry pot overturn and all the shirts being washed to fall into the mud?"

He sighed. "No, Pothwen and his idiot dog did that. . . . Ailis, you haven't answered my question."

After a while, since she showed no signs of responding and simply sat and combed out her hair, Gerard got up, threw an oiled cloth over his head to keep away the worst of the rain, and went outside. He came back a little while later carrying the evening meal; two bowls of surprisingly good stew from the communal cook-pot, only slightly diluted by rain.

"Better than making either one of us do the cooking," he said as he handed her a bowl, referring to their various burned or undercooked meals while on the road together in the past. Gerard was a terrible cook, Newt was even worse, and Ailis was only slightly better than the two of them.

"It's warm. That's what counts." She put down her comb and found spoons.

"I don't understand why you have to do that," he said finally.

"Do what?" Ailis was at a loss, having forgotten where their conversation had ended.

"Use magic," Gerard clarified.

She put down her spoon and stared at him. "Why do you use a sword?"

"That's different," he protested.

"You're right. It is. A sword is just a tool. Magic is what I am. *Who* I am. If you have trouble with that, then you have trouble with me." Her eyes glistened, but in the candlelight he couldn't tell if it was from anger or tears.

"Ailis. Stop that. Please."

He didn't often say "please." In fact, she couldn't remember the last time he had said it.

"I just can't understand why you don't see how dangerous it might be," he said, looking down into his stew.

"Dangerous for who? For me?" She really did have to laugh at that. "Ger, I'm not doing anything big. Nothing important. Just little spells to keep myself ready."

He looked up at that. "Ready for what?"

"Anything that might need magic," she replied matter-of-factly. "Ger, do you stop practicing your swordplay just because the king has made treaties with the countries around us?"

"Don't be—no." He saw the trap closing around him, but couldn't back out of it.

"So?"

"It's not the same," he said again, more weakly this time. "Magic is different. It's dangerous. . . . Unpredictable."

"All the more reason for me to learn how to control it. The same way you learn how to use your sword. Or do you want me to be entirely defenseless? Is that it? Even Merlin—"

"Even Merlin what?" Gerard pounced on her words like a cat on a rat.

"Nothing."

"Ailis, did Merlin tell you not to do magic?"

"No," she said defiantly. "In fact, he said I *should* keep practicing. Discreetly."

"And you call this discreet?" With a wave of his hand, he indicated the storm outside.

"You're just upset because we're not going to be moving out in the morning the way Sir Matthias wanted, which means that another group might find the Grail first." She shook her head. Her hair was completely dry by now, and the long, dark red strands streamed down her back in a rumpled cascade. "I told you when the king first started this—the Grail's not a thing to be won. It has to be earned. And if you ask me, there's not a man on this entire Quest who's earned it."

"So you *did* cause this storm." He declared, triumphant. They were back in familiar territory now. Ailis and Gerard had been squabbling like this, on different topics, since they were children.

Ailis looked as though she wanted very badly to throw her bowl of stew at him. Familiar also meant that they knew exactly where to hit to accomplish the most damage. "Why are you so tangled up in the thought of me using magic? I could understand it from Newt, but you—you know that magic isn't bad! It's not evil!"

"It's Sir Matthias. He thinks . . ." Gerard really didn't want to go on, but he had started, so there was no dropping it now.

"What about him?"

"He thinks that magic profanes the Quest."

"He what?"

Gerard looked miserable. He was not only carrying tales, but making trouble, when all he wanted to do was warn Ailis. "He thinks that magic . . . that it's wrong to use on the Quest. And if he finds out that you've been using it, I'm worried he'll—"

"He'll what? Toss me out by the side of the road—to fend for myself?"

"Of course not!" That would be wrong. Unchivalrous. And it would deeply disturb both Arthur and Merlin, who had chosen to send Ailis out with the Quest.

"Good. Because Merlin sent me on this journey in order to use my skill to help find the Grail, remember?"

"When the time was right, as I recall." Gerard

was also remembering a discussion he and Merlin and Newt had had before Ailis rejoined them. They talked over their concerns about the influence Morgain might have had on the girl; about what traps the enchantress might have set, waiting for Ailis to trigger them. Ailis was part of the Quest for many reasons, not the least of which was to see if she drew Morgain to her. But that was one secret that Gerard would rather die than divulge to her.

"All I am saying is . . . be careful. Don't . . . don't play around with magic. Don't cause storms, or . . . or do anything. Just . . ."

"Just sit in a corner and do needlework and look pretty for the knights? Is that what you're saying?" Ailis stood up, slamming her thankfully now empty bowl onto the ground.

"I am so very tired of everyone telling me to sit, and wait, and be a good girl! 'You'll have your time,' Morgain says. 'The time is coming,' Merlin says. 'Don't do anything to draw attention to yourself,' you say. Why not? Why must everything be hidden under a rock? When do *I* get to stand up and take credit for helping to defeat Morgain, rather than just hiding behind you and Newt and your swords and your bashing?"

Her hands balled up at her sides as though she wanted to hit something, and the words poured out of her.

"Morgain was right about one thing—nobody takes me seriously! Not even Merlin! Everyone tells me what I can't do, and nobody wants to see what I *can* do! Nobody—except Newt." She saw Gerard flinch and went for the kill, not knowing why, except that it was effective and she was angry.

"Newt's scared of magic, but he doesn't tell me not to use it. He doesn't tell me to sit in a corner and act like a lady, or not to speak to anyone, and not to wear pants, or—"

She knew it wasn't fair. Gerard had never said those things to her. It wasn't his fault Sir Matthias wanted her to be a substitute for his delicate daughter. And Newt wasn't all that accepting of her, either. He wanted to keep an eye out for her, reminding her of how useless she was without the magic, and how, if it wasn't for the magic, she would never have met Morgain. And then she never would have had her eyes opened to all the possibilities in the world—the possibilities that everyone kept holding out of her reach, telling her "not yet."

"Ailis—"

"No!"

As she shouted it, an unexpected clash of thunder split the heavens. They both stopped and stared at each other.

"I didn't make the storm," she said in a much quieter voice. "But I can make it stop. That should make everyone happy, right? And nobody will ever know. Just the way you all want it."

She turned and stalked out into the rain, not bothering with her shoes or jacket or the oiled tarp.

Gerard sighed, picked up his stew bowl, and started eating his dinner. If she was going to be like that, there was nothing he could do to stop her.

*   *   *

Elsewhere in the camp, Newt had his hands full with a different kind of argument.

During the storm, one of the flimsier pavilions had blown over, exposing a knight's belongings to the weather and resulting in the hapless squire responsible having his ears boxed.

Newt had come along while the boy and two of his friends were trying to get the fabric back up, while the knight took refuge with a neighbor, drinking wine and watching the boys struggle.

"Fine example of chivalry," Newt had said, but only to himself. Out loud, he had ordered the smallest boy to collect all of the objects still lying in the grass and place them under a small, oiled tarp.

Meanwhile, he and the two other boys began replacing pegs, careful not to trip over or stumble into any of the neighboring tents in the dark. The rain finally let up just as he was about to tell them to bring out the top-most fabric. They were able to unfold the cloth and set the ropes without too much difficulty, despite the lack of light beyond the torches the knights had put up.

"Down, boy," Newt said now, holding his hand at hip level to illustrate what he wanted, the way he would if working with a half-trained dog. His voice was soothing, gentle, and shaking with laughter, as he teased the younger boy who held the other end of the rope.

"Grrrr." The boy at the other end of the rope bared his teeth and growled, but obediently went down onto his knees in order to tie the rope to the peg without losing any of the tautness.

"You pull a good rope," one of the squires called. "Pity it's bound to end up around your neck."

Newt laughed and went to the third rope, making

sure it had been tied properly. There were few things you learned faster working in the kennels, the way he had as a young boy, than how to tie a secure knot.

"Up the tent!" Newt called, and they hauled on the ropes until the pavilion cover was upright once again.

"Good, dog-boy!" one of the squires called, continuing the rough-handed teasing. "Say woof!"

"That's horse-boy to you, and I say to you 'neigh.'"

"Four legs, a tail, and no brains—not so much of a difference between horse and dog."

"You take that back!"

Newt looked up from tying off the final rope only to see the squire flat on his back in the mud, Gerard looming over him, holding him down. "You don't speak to him like that—not until you've done as much as he has," Gerard growled.

"Ger!" Newt knew that Gerard had a temper— he had, in fact, been at the receiving end of it many times—but this seemed extreme. "Gerard, it's okay!" He hauled Gerard off the now muddy squire, shoving him, gently, to arms' distance away.

"What was that all about?"

"He said—"

"I heard what he said."

"He—it doesn't bother you?" Gerard looked at Newt, then up at the now clear sky as though there might be some answer up there.

"It would have if it meant anything." Newt knew that he had sore spots, things that riled him when poked, but he very rarely got angry. His mother had taught him to let things slide off his shoulders, and working with animals sensitive to your moods had set the lessons in stone. Anger had no place in his life, especially over such a foolish thing as name-calling.

"I appreciate the championship," Newt said. "But I don't need it."

He was tired of Gerard always playing the squire role no matter what, as though that were the only thing that mattered. He was tired of hiding his participation in events, of staying quiet in order to keep any rumor or hint of trouble at Camelot from spreading.

"If you'd fought like that when we first met, you might actually have won," he said instead.

"If Sir Lancelot hadn't shown up to save you, you'd have been wearing your face backward," Gerard retorted, reaching to help the squire he'd just tackled up from the mud. "Callum, isn't it?"

"Yes."

"Sorry about that, Callum. Newt's a friend of mine, and I don't take well to him being mocked. Even in jest."

"I'll remember that." The boy was unhappy, but clearly unable to find fault either with Gerard's apology, or his reasoning.

Gerard glanced up at the sky, then turned to Newt, his face serious again. "We need to talk about Ailis."

"Ailis? Is she all right?" Newt looked around, as though expecting to see her in the crowd gathering around them.

Gerard looked up at the sky again and found the moon that was beginning to rise. "We need to talk," was all he said.

"Gather!"

The call came from the center of camp, and everyone turned to hear who was yelling.

"Gather!"

"That's Tom," Gerard said, relieved at the interruption. Tom was Sir Matthias's squire, the one who actually *was* stuck polishing gear and minding the horses. "Something must have happened. Come on!"

The two friends pushed through the crowd, slipping occasionally on the mud-slick grass, to where Sir Matthias was standing. A young, nervous-looking monk was beside him. There were torches set up to hold the darkness at bay, but even with them, everything had a strange, shadowy cast. It caused Newt to look around nervously, waiting for something to jump out at them.

"Nobody else feels it."

"What?" Gerard said.

Ailis had appeared next to Newt, looking straight ahead, watching not Sir Matthias, but the monk with him. "The darkness. Nobody else feels it."

"*You* do." Newt's words were less a statement than a question.

"So do you, don't you?" Ailis said, looking at Newt closely. They were feeling the same strange tension in the air, a tension which seemed to be increasing, rather than fading.

Gerard had stopped listening to them. Instead he watched Sir Matthias and the monk.

"Which means . . . ?" Newt wasn't sure what he was asking.

"I don't know. There's something about that

monk. The darkness, it has been placed on him, somehow, as though . . ."

"Shhhh," Gerard hushed them as Sir Matthias began to speak.

"This is Brother Jannot. He—"

"The Grail hides." The monk had a deep voice, deeper than his body should have been able to produce, and it carried even into the darkness. "The Grail hides in shadows, in long dark shadows. Bring the light, and dispel the shadows. Find the Grail."

"A prophecy," one of the knights muttered. "He's been gifted with the art of prophecy."

"A miracle," another said. "The voice of God speaks through him!"

Slowly, the mood of the gathered men changed from irritation and exhaustion to exultation, with Sir Matthias and the now silent monk at the heart of it. Even Gerard and Newt got caught up in the energy, Newt totally forgetting his earlier unease.

Only Ailis, pushed to the side by the crowd of people trying to get close enough to touch the monk's robe, looked distressed, not uplifted, by the prophecy.

"Something's wrong," she whispered, feeling it in her bones, in her blood. There was a sense of the world being twisted somehow. She could feel it, taste it, in the monk's words.

But nobody heard her; everyone was so caught up in the monk's revelation. He gave them exactly what they wanted to hear.

THREE

The next morning found them riding out of sunlit fields and into a dark, shadowed forest. The road narrowed so that they could not ride more than three abreast. The supply wagon came perilously close to overrunning the cleared area and tipping into the narrow rainwater-carved ditch on one side.

"I don't like this." Ailis kept looking back over her shoulder, her hand reaching to stroke her horse's neck for reassurance. The gelding was one of Arthur's own with the royal brand on its hindquarters. It was trained to carry messengers, lads about Ailis's size and weight. That familiar weight, Newt had said, would keep the horse calm and steady no matter how far they traveled, or under what conditions. So far that had been true, and Ailis was thankful for it. She was a better rider now than she had ever dreamed of being before all this began, but it still wasn't natural to her the way it was for the boys.

"Which *this* would that be?" Gerard asked. "The fact that we're chasing after a rumor based on something a half-mad monk said, the fact that we're riding into a big dark forest everyone calls the Shadows, because the word has 'shadow' in its name, or—"

"Or because everyone around here says that this forest is haunted with evil spirits?" Newt added.

"I don't believe in ghosties," Callum said stoutly, but he was a little paler than normal as he looked around nervously. He'd chosen to ride with them this morning, despite or perhaps because of the fight the night before. His mount, a delicate-boned mare with a lovely gait, was taking her cue from him, shying and snorting at every bird or small beast that moved. Newt would have felt sorrier, except for Callum's stubborn determination to outdo Gerard in every way, including his casual disregard for anything not sword or shield. It was annoying enough to have one adventure-hungry squire around—two was *exhausting*.

Newt didn't like magic. He didn't trust magic. But he wasn't fool enough to deny it existed. He'd never seen a ghost before. But he'd seen a dragon, a bridge troll, a sea serpent . . . after that, unquiet spirits weren't so difficult to imagine.

"Why would the Grail be hidden in a forest?" Ailis asked for the seventh or eighth time since Sir Matthias had announced their destination that morning.

"Why would the Grail be hidden anywhere?" Newt asked, feeling the urge to be difficult. He wanted to show Gerard and Ailis that they weren't the only ones with brains. "Why not just leave it in a house of worship on an altar, have something built for it to show it off for the true believers. . . ."

"Because it's too powerful to be left in plain sight." In the morning sun, Gerard looked as exhausted as Newt felt—Sir Matthias had had him running all night after the monk's revelation, ensuring that everyone would be ready to leave first thing in the morning.

"And it is especially too powerful to put in a house of worship, with access given to men of faith—men to whom the power of the Grail might be an eternal temptation." Callum was green, but not stupid.

"So it makes sense to hide it," Newt said, his agreement clearly confusing to Callum and Gerard. Ailis, he noted, was shooting him a look that said she knew what he was doing, and while she was amused, she didn't quite approve. Their bickering felt familiar.

It felt like comfort. It felt like *family*.

"And to hide it somewhere with a reputation, so nobody will come looking, poking around . . ." he continued, despite her look.

"Somewhere with a reputation that would explain anything strange that might happen around such a powerful object!" Gerard finished the thought triumphantly.

"I hate it when you two make sense." Ailis managed a faint imitation of her old, cheerful smile. "Fortunately it doesn't happen often."

In the daylight, with the mud, confusion, and lack of direction left behind them in the old encampment, the three friends plus Callum, who seemed to have attached himself to Newt, were able to pick up some of the anticipation, if not the high spirits, of the rest of their caravan. It was enough, at least, to bring back some of their old banter, the back and forth that had gotten them through difficult times before.

There was an edge to it now though, one that Newt was slowly becoming aware of, mostly from Ailis: She was sharper, more brittle with Gerard, as though trying to defend herself against attacks that never actually came. He wished he could feel more regret for that, but instead found himself taking advantage of it, agreeing with Ailis more obviously, just to rile his friend and see the flash of gratitude on her face. He knew it was small and petty, but he didn't stop doing it.

"Did you see that?" Ailis asked suddenly.

"See what?"

If Callum were any more fidgety, Newt thought, he was going to twitch himself right out of his saddle.

"Behind Sir Matthias," she said, indicating the direction with her chin, so as to not be too obvious about it. Newt looked but couldn't see anything in the forest.

The knight in question reined in his horse—a great muscled beast—from the front of the line letting his knights continue on past him. Then he walked the massive charger back to where the four of them were riding.

"Gerard." He acknowledged the others with a nod of his head, but his attention was solely on the older squire. "We will be coming to the place the monk spoke of, perhaps by midday. I will want to camp there, at least until we have some sense of where the Grail might be. I want you to take the northwest quadrant of camp, make sure it is set up properly, and let me know if there are any problems."

It was an important job for a squire. Gerard sat up proudly in his saddle despite the weight of this responsibility.

"Sir, I—" Ailis began, then stopped when Sir Matthias turned a gentle eye on her.

"My dear, I want you to promise me you'll stay close to one of the squires at all times. This is a rough place, and I would not wish to regret allowing you to come with us." He patted her kindly on the cheek then, with another nod to Gerard, turned his horse and rode back to the front of the line.

The good mood among the four of them had been broken. Ailis was fuming once again, the paternal warning another reminder that she was only a girl and therefore of no use to the Quest.

Meanwhile, Callum felt slighted not only by Sir Matthias's focus on Gerard, but by the dismissal of his new hero, Newt. Gerard, basking in the trust given him by the brave knight, was aware of their dissatisfaction but, not knowing how to deal with it, chose to ignore it instead.

"You saw something?" he said to Ailis.

"Never mind," she said. "It's gone now. It was probably just a haunt, nothing that would bother a mighty warrior like him, who doesn't have to worry about things not of the mortal, *ordinary* world."

"Ailis . . ."

She just looked at him, daring him to push the matter. He sighed, letting it drop.

"Hoy!"

Two of the other squires rode up alongside them, waving to Callum. With a sideways glance at Newt, the younger squire peeled away from their group, clearly pleased to be leaving the sudden tension to rejoin his old companions.

"Horse-boy!" one of them called. "You, too!"

Newt didn't hesitate turning his horse off the path to join the three waiting for him. He didn't particularly want to spend time with the rougher-edged squires, whose idea of fun was uncomfortably close to that of the dogs he used to tend. But anything was better than sitting between Gerard and Ailis when they were upset with each other, as seemed to be the case too often these days.

"Ailis . . ." Gerard tried again. "I'm sorry. Sir Matthias is so . . ." he floundered, looking for a word. "Old-fashioned," he said, finally. "He doesn't believe . . ."

"No, he doesn't," she said shortly. "And neither do you, apparently." She would have ridden off, but unlike Newt and Callum she had nowhere else to go. Instead, she settled for watching the tall, dark-columned trees that lined the narrow road, noting with great intensity the colors of the leaves, the texture of the bark, and where it had been eaten away by deer and other grazers. And all the while the sense of something just out of sight, something following them, persisted. That and the eerie feeling she'd had during the monk's prophecy . . .

"Don't bring attention to yourself," Merlin had said. "Stay quiet and out of sight." If she brought her suspicions to Sir Matthias's attention, she would have to explain why and how she knew what she knew— and that would involve mentioning Morgain. And Ailis wasn't *certain*, after all . . . so she said nothing.

* * *

Newt was dizzy. The whirlwind of the past several days swam through his mind. His feet were slightly uncertain as he walked under the trees back to his bedroll.

There was no room to erect the pavilions of the previous camp, but tarps had been raised, and some semblance of comfort established. Many of the squires had decided to sleep under their masters' roofs while they were in the Shadows, but Newt preferred the fresh air, even if he couldn't see the sky through the thick branches overhead. The trees between him and the main camp gave him the illusion of privacy, something he had missed since leaving his horse-charges back at Camelot.

"*Chhhhheeereeeee.*"

So far tonight, he had heard three different calls, none of which he had encountered before. Some might claim the howls and whoops were the voices of unrestful souls, but Newt knew they were merely night-birds, flitting and hunting low overhead.

He came to the open space in the center of four great tree trunks where his bedroll had been placed. Callum had left a small fire burning in the fire pit, and Newt held back a sigh of exasperation. The boy should have known enough to bank the flames before he fell asleep, especially in such a densely wooded area.

Newt stepped over Callum's blanket-covered form and went to rearrange the wood so that the flames would die down again, leaving only smoldering coals that could be restarted come morning.

As he bent over the flames, he heard another noise, this one more of a yelping sound—the sort a fox kit might make when excited or alarmed. Only it was too narrow and thready to be a fox's call. Newt looked over his shoulder into the night-dark surroundings, but saw no telltale glow of eyes, and heard no rustle of leaves that might indicate the passing of such a creature. Callum slept through it all, not even shifting at the disturbance.

Foxes, no matter how odd-sounding, were neither interesting enough nor worrisome enough to keep Newt from his bed any longer—not after a long day of riding. So without further hesitation, he slid off his boots and jerkin, put them within reach, and went to sleep.

*   *   *

Sir Thomas wiped a cloth across the toe of his boot and admired the shine, then looked up as Gerard walked by. "Ho, Gerard! You weren't at the fire last night."

Gerard paused when the young knight called his name, and said, "No." After dinner the knights and squires had gathered to share stories. Sir Matthias encouraged it, to a certain level.

Gerard had wanted to join in, but he was still smarting a little from the comments made during the day's ride, and the thought of dealing with Newt and Callum, both of whom were part of the gathering, had seemed too much to bear. Instead he had taken a turn around the campsite, so spread out as to barely deserve the name, and then gone to bed.

"Pity. Sir Ruden was telling us stories of the Northern Campaign, when Merlin tamed that so-called monster and banished it to the lake."

"It was a monster, nothing so-called about it!" Sir Ruden had a thick northern accent, but his indignation was clear. "Ah, that was an adventure, it was. Not like this." He spat once, indicating his opinion of the Quest.

"We're about to do some training with swords before Sir Matthias decides to move us out again," Sir Thomas went on. "Care to join us?"

"Us" was Sir Thomas, Sir Ruden, who was from the Highlands, Sir Brand, and Sir Daffyd, both of whom were from Camelot proper.

Sir Brand and Sir Daffyd were also two of the least-experienced knights on the Quest and, in Gerard's opinion, not the sharpest men in the group. But they were knights.

Thomas had been made a knight only just before the Quest rode out. Gerard had, in fact, worked with him years ago, when both their masters were at Camelot at the same time. Thomas had not been in Camelot when the sleep-spell was cast. If he had been, perhaps Gerard would not have been the oldest squire left awake in the castle, and perhaps none of what had followed would have happened at all.

Thomas didn't seem to hold this against Gerard. He was secure in the status of his newly granted spurs, polished and gleaming against his boots. Not that there had been very much glory: Merlin and Arthur had specifically asked Gerard not to speak to the other knights about his adventures, for fear of raising the very doubts and questions about Arthur's kingship that Morgain had intended to create by her spells.

"All right, let's get started," Sir Brand said, getting into his saddle. He reached down for the long, blunted lance Daffyd handed him. "Thomas, you and Gerard—"

"Oh, please!"

At the sound of a woman's voice, Gerard spun around, even as his ears told him that it wasn't Ailis. The voice was too high, too breathy, too delicate.

"Please, good sirs, help me."

She was tiny, barely as tall as Gerard's shoulder,

with a round, flushed face and a mass of dark curly hair that had twigs and leaves in it, as though she had just come crashing through the undergrowth.

"Milady?" Thomas said, gallant as though he were the eldest of King Arthur's knights, and not the latest and most recent. She was no lady—her drab homespun kirtle and scuffed boots made that clear— but her distress was real, and the knights responded to that exactly as they had been trained.

"Milady, how may we help you?"

"My village. Back that way," and she waved a vague hand northward. "Terrible—terrible!" Her nut-brown eyes were bloodshot and showed tremendous fear, lending force to her jumbled, breathless words. Her hands, scratched and bleeding, rose to clutch at Sir Ruden's sleeve, as he leaned down from the back of his horse to hear her words better.

"Save us," she pleaded. "Only you, with your swords, can save us."

No sweeter balm ever landed on their ears, the perfect antidote to their failure to discover the Grail.

"Milady, we will," Brand vowed, offering his hand to draw the girl up onto his horse.

She pulled back, clearly afraid of the beast. Instead she turned and, lifting her skirt a little to move more easily, said "I beg you, follow me." And with that, she ran off toward the villages.

Gerard and Thomas hauled themselves up and into their saddles, their horses already moving to keep up with the others, and rode off after her.

"We shouldn't just leave," Gerard said, the thought coming belatedly that maybe this wasn't something Sir Matthias would be pleased about. "We should tell someone where we're going, get more men . . ."

"You're right—you go tell Sir Matthias—you're his boy, after all," Daffyd said unkindly. "Leave the glory to the men."

Laughter trailed back as the others heard that. Gerard's mouth tightened as common sense warred with his pride. It took only a moment before common sense was bashed over the head and left in the bushes. Gerard rode after the knights.

The girl clearly knew where she was leading them, a path seeming to open up where Gerard had seen none before. In no time at all, they were riding out of the trees' embrace and saw before them a small, neatly tended village, surrounded on two sides by fields.

In the early morning mist, the timber-cut houses

and sheds seemed to glisten, the green patches of garden looked ready to burst with late-harvest pro-duce, and even the occasional dog looked placid and well-fed enough not to bark at the sudden arrival of strangers on horseback.

It was, Gerard thought, a lovely picture. But it was too quiet to be the scene of such danger—unless they were too late.

"What sort of threat do we face?" he asked the girl, who had stopped to stare at the village with a sort of pained fascination.

"Go, quickly, swiftly," she said, not quite in response to his question. "Swiftly, you may yet save us."

The knights needed no further urging. They spurred their horses into a trot, loosened their swords from their scabbards, and readied smaller blades. Sir Thomas pulled a long dagger from a sheath strapped between his shoulder blades—placed there for easy access while riding—and grinned with anticipation of what could prove to be his first true test as a knight.

In earlier years, Gerard might have charged in, front and center, thrilled to be with these young knights, excited to face battle, determined to rescue innocents. But his travels had changed him in ways he hadn't realized until now, and second thoughts tugged at him.

Newt had shown him that appearances weren't always truth. Ailis reminded him over and over that even familiar, ordinary things can change suddenly. Arthur's need to be in so many places at once taught him the importance of evaluating threats. Morgain—and her magics—had shown him that danger comes in all forms, shapes, and sizes, and from any direction at all.

"Wait!" he called, reining in his horse, but the others had already gone on ahead, riding now at a full gallop into the village itself.

And still none of the dogs barked.

Gerard turned on the girl, now beside him. "What have you led us to? What are you—" His voice dried up and stuck in his throat.

Her hair had sprouted leaves, her skin turned from buttermilk to bark-brown, and her hands—the fingers were too long, had too many joints; they looked like twigs, not flesh.

"Wood-witch!" he cried, dismayed. Of all the dangers of a haunted forest, this was one he had never thought to beware: a poppet made from an ensorcelled tree or brush, animated and given life by evil magics, controlled by the creator and used to cause mischief . . . or lead men to disaster.

He looked up again, just in time to see the sleepy dogs begin to move. Not getting to their feet, or acting in familiar ways, but . . . they moved. They shook and quivered, until their bodies broke apart and *things* ran out of them. Gerard pushed his horse forward, fighting to keep control of the now skittish beast, who was clearly unnerved by a smell, something sharp and bitter and unnatural, that the changing breeze brought from the village.

The wood-witch had disappeared back into the forest, but Gerard couldn't spare any attention for her, not with what was unfolding in front of him.

The creatures seemed harmless at first. About the size of Gerard's palm, they moved like spiders, skittish on multiple legs. A grown man—or a horse—could stomp them into splinters, taken individually or even a dozen at a time. But there were so many of them pouring out of the dogs' bodies that the ground looked like a black stream from dogs to knights.

"Beware!" The words came from Gerard's mouth without conscious thought. "Look out behind you!"

Part of Gerard wanted nothing more than to flee,

to lash his horse into the fastest run it could manage, scooping Ailis up behind him, yelling for Newt, and having Ailis open a gateway back to Camelot— ideally directly into Merlin's chambers.

Even as he was wishing that he could do all that, a cold, practical part of him was moving closer. He was still far enough away to avoid triggering an attack on himself, but near enough that he could see what was happening. He had to know, had to be able to make a full report . . . *And if they catch me? Who will make a report then?* The coward's voice asked, trying to justify its fear. *Let's go, let's get out of here!*

Gerard forced that thought into oblivion, even as he felt the cold sweat dripping down his back and along the tops of his arms.

It's all right to be frightened. The trick is not to let the fear rule you. A faint memory spoke, a lingering trace, perhaps, of the blood-spell Merlin had worked on them, giving them access to his wisdom and Arthur's experience. Or maybe by now it was his own voice. Either way, the knowledge steadied him into doing what had to be done.

Sir Brand and Sir Daffyd had already dismounted, swords in their hands, when the spider-things appeared. Sir Ruden and Thomas were mounted, and their horses reared and shied away first, alerting them that something was wrong even as Gerard shouted his warning.

And then the creatures were swarming the four knights, covering them, their armor, swords, even daggers were useless. Brand disappeared under a wave of black, then Daffyd fell to the ground as though stunned. Thomas tried to spur his horse out of the way, but the things were moving up the horse's legs now, and the horse shrieked, a huge, painful sound. It fell onto its side, lather poured from its mouth, and Thomas was likewise covered. Ruden sprang from the saddle and tried to run on foot. He looked up and saw Gerard, at least temporarily out of harm's way.

"Run! Flee!" he shouted, and then he, too, was taken down by the creatures.

Poison, Gerard thought. They had to give off a poison, by bite or sting that stunned their victims. He had no idea what sort of creature could do that to a full-grown man or horse . . . other than something magical.

And that was perhaps the most foolish thought he'd ever had in his entire life. Of *course* it was something magical.

The tiny black things abandoned Brand, leaving behind a figure crisscrossed by shimmering white threads, like some kind of spiderweb spun of moonlight. But from the way Brand struggled uselessly against it, Gerard had to assume it was stronger than spider silk or moonshine. Thomas was next, then Ruden. The more they struggled, the more tightly they were bound. Ruden saw that and seemed to submit to his fate, allowing them to bind him.

"Lad!" Ruden called out to him, his voice weak behind the net but no less commanding. "Come, help us! Set us free!"

Against his better judgment, Gerard dismounted, patting the horse on its crest, soothing it as best he could. He studied a nearby tree cautiously, wondering if it, too, was enchanted in some way, then took the chance and tied his horse's reins to a low-hanging branch. The slipknot was secure enough so that he wouldn't have to worry about chasing after the foolish beast if it bolted, but not so firmly the beast couldn't flee if the spiderlike things came after it.

Gerard really didn't want to think about that. If the creatures went after his horse, it would mean that he had already been . . . consumed.

As he inched closer, ready with every step to flee

back to safety, it looked as though the creatures were in no hurry to eat their captives or the horses, which had fallen motionless on the earth. Instead, the things were turning on their smaller brothers, binding and consuming them in messy gulps.

Better they eat each other. Fewer to fight, when it comes to that.

Gerard made his way another length closer, then another. Several of the creatures paused long enough to rotate beady-eyed heads in his direction, and Gerard shuddered under their scrutiny. He forced himself to remain still and eventually they turned back to their gruesome actions.

"Lad. *Gerard.* Can you free us?"

Sir Ruden was the only one who seemed able to speak clearly. Sir Brand was clearly unconscious, and Daffyd was facedown on the ground, not moving beyond the faintest rising and falling of his chest as he breathed. Sir Thomas kept struggling against his bonds, to the point where his mouth was muffled by the ever-tightening bands.

"Stop that, or it will cut off your air," Sir Ruden said, as sharply as a whisper could manage, then returned his attention to Gerard. "Can you?"

"I . . . don't think so." He *wanted* to be the hero,

72

but the practical voice was in charge. Even moving a handspan closer meant attracting the attention of the spiders, and he still had no idea what might fend them off. He considered fire but had no means to make any. Water? Most villages were near a stream or creek, but he didn't hear rushing water anywhere. Even so, without a bucket he couldn't do anything, and going into the village to get a bucket would not be wise. The moment he crossed over, he would be bound and imprisoned the same as the others.

"No, sir," he said finally. "I don't think I can."

Silence fell, emphasizing the faint crunching and sucking noises of the feeding spiders. It made Gerard's skin prickle again. To distract himself, he looked more closely at the spider silk, trying to see if there was a break or a pattern he had missed. With a jolt of horror, he realized that the leather gear the four of them were wearing, basic traveling armor, was beginning to dissolve under the pressure of the bonds. A glance back at Sir Ruden showed that he was aware of what was going on, as well.

"*Go.*" Sir Ruden, his eyes dark through the white ties binding him, stared at Gerard as though by that alone he could move the boy. "Find Matthias . . . return . . ."

Gerard hesitated, torn. Part of honor demanded loyalty and he could not leave his companions there helpless.

Leaving them seemed like betrayal. But to go closer would be to end up with the same fate.

With a heavy heart, Gerard took off.

FOUR

"Lovely. Simply lovely."

They were horrible beasts, the blood-spiders, but Morgain could understand her companion's satisfaction in their work. Only a dozen, placed on the outskirts of a village, could reproduce in an afternoon to become a veritable army. Of course, they needed to be fed after that, but every plan had a cost.

And Morgain hadn't had any supporters in that village, anyway, and did not have much to lose.

When her spies reported that some of Arthur's knights had taken her prophetic "gift" and were moving into the Shadows, Morgain had uttered the spell which released the blood-spiders. Then she had given them the image of a knight in traveling gear. The moment after one of them saw a knight, they would all cease feeding and hold the intruders.

And so it had happened. The monk's prophecy twisted to her own means had been the trigger, Morgain's handcrafted wood-witch had been the bait, and the spiders the jaws of the trap.

A deep bell chimed from somewhere deep within the keep. The shadow-figure, garbed once again in a heavy hooded robe, turned as though responding to something below the tones, something beyond Morgain's hearing. The great hooded head nodded once, and a slender, white-skinned hand was raised to tap Morgain once on the shoulder.

"I need to be here," she said.

"You do not. The araneae will do as they were created to do. The plan has been set in motion, and it cannot be stopped now. Come." The words were spoken in a gentle voice, but they had an undeniable force behind them. Morgain resisted, tapping her fingers on the surface of the flat-edged scrying crystal, then relented. Pushing back in her chair, she waved her hand over the crystal and uttered a silent command. The crystal flickered, then went blank. She had set a spell to keep anything from coming in—or going out. If not monitored, a scry might be used by others wishing to see in, as well—a sort of magical peephole for invaders. Unlike the sometimes scatterbrained Merlin, she never left her flanks unguarded.

Morgain was able to keep up easily with her companion, her wool dress allowing her full stride. Despite her outward confidence, however, a strange sensation filled her. Part of it was anticipation: Whatever the shadow-figure was ready to show her would be the result of three years of planning. These were long years, filled with setbacks and failures, small successes and a seemingly endless supply of patience. Part of what she was feeling, however, was fear.

But Morgain did not allow fear to motivate her. It simply was not an acceptable emotion. Fear was a weakness to be exploited in others, not allowed in herself. Fear makes one doubt, hesitate.

She had no doubts. No hesitations.

If this was to be as she hoped, then she would adapt it, and move on. There was no failure, not so long as she breathed. It was not the possibility of failure that made Morgain's breath hitch and her pulse stutter. Rather, it was the awareness that she was, for the first time since she was a child, allowing another to guide her actions. The ghostlike companion was the architect of this particular scheme; she had only a limited role in its creation, for all that she was the cause, the guiding force.

Morgain was not accustomed to not being in control. But to accomplish what her companion promised—a way to humiliate Merlin and to keep Arthur from getting his bloody, Romanized hands on the Grail—she would be willing to compromise. Even give up some control. For a little while.

Down they went, around a spiral staircase, through a doorway cut into the rocky wall, and down another staircase, this one without railings or visible support. It led to a large stone room, deep inside the keep. The entire building breathed around them, resting its weight on the walls and supports. This was one of four such underground rooms, deep in the bedrock upon which her home was built.

Safe. Secure. To all intents magical and practical, invisible.

In the center of the otherwise bare chamber, there was a wooden table, similar to the one in her workroom, only three times the size, to match the scale of the room. It was covered with a heavy cloth made of the same material as her companion's robes.

"It is done."

At another time, there would have been satisfaction in those words, or pride, or even relief. The companion's voice was purely matter-of-fact.

"Let me see," Morgain demanded.

Invisible hands pulled the cloth back without flourish, revealing a map spread out on the table, covering its entire surface. At first glance, it looked to be merely a larger version of the map upstairs in Morgain's workroom, without the lights moving upon it, but there was much more vivid, intense detail. The still waters of the ocean were almost life-like in the way it glistened, and each individual stalk of wheat seemed ready to sway in the breeze, waiting only for the peasants to begin harvesting.

Morgain leaned over the map, looking closely, and was so beguiled that when her companion seized her arm, she was taken by surprise. Even more so when the blade appeared in its slender fingers, the sharp edge scoring a narrow, bloodless line up the inside of her arm.

"What?" It didn't hurt, but the shock was enough to make her voice rise.

Even as she protested, the companion's strong fingers had released her. Morgain pulled her arm away, inspecting the damage. As she did, a single drop of blood rose from the cut and then fell, as though slowed by forces beyond magic.

It hit the surface, breaking into dozens of minuscule droplets, and splattered across the trees, fields, and buildings.

And the shadow-figure said, again, "It is done."

This time, Morgain felt a change in the air around them. Drawn to the source, the sorceress looked down. The map, formerly only lifelike, had actually come to life. Waves crashed against the shoreline, birds soared in the air, animals slogged in the fields and pens, and the tiny forms of people moved within their villages, their limbs all powered by some usurpation of nature.

Morgain's pale skin drained even further of color, and her teeth were bared in an expression that could never be mistaken for a smile. *Her blood*. Her companion had used *her blood* to create this mockery.

"The trap has been set," the shadow-figure said, as though reading her mind. "Your blood was needed to bait it, to set it in motion. But it is the girl's blood which will trigger it. *Her* blood, which Merlin has tampered with, touched with his own, and Arthur's as well, that gives us the key to them both."

Morgain didn't bother to ask for further explanation; she knew that it was just the sort of headstrong thing Merlin would do, to tamper with children in that manner. And Arthur would know no better. This was a good trap, well-made, one Morgain herself would not have been able to escape, connected as she was to Arthur through their blood ties. And if Ailis did indeed have connections to both wizard and king, then so much the better. Then the most powerful beings in Camelot would both be pulled in and trapped inside, leaving Morgain free to step into their space.

But Morgain thought of Ailis . . . thought of risking the witch-child, her would-be student, her protégée . . .

"How dare you," she said, fury turning her words to ice. "How *dare* you use her?"

She moved forward, her body language screaming her intent to destroy the map. She stopped suddenly; it was as though a wall had appeared in front of her, blocking her path.

"This is what you asked for. This is what I gave you. There is no turning back."

Morgain glared at the map, which glinted with seemingly innocent, still-inert magics.

"Do you know what you have done?" she asked, her voice still bitter, her gaze unwavering, unblinking. The map was more than a picture now; it was the land itself. To close the trap, more than a drop of Ailis's blood would be required. She would have to be drained dry.

"All magic has a cost. All bargains must be sealed with blood. You knew this, Morgain, Enchantress, daughter of Morgause, Queen of Orkney. Take what is given and use it to accomplish your goals. Do not flinch from the cost."

The words might not be pleasant, but that made them no less true. Morgain forced the tension and anger from her body, and made herself look at the map, not as betrayal, but possibility. There was always a cost, but it did not always have to be paid the same way.

FIVE

Branches scratched at Gerard's face and arms as he rode through the underbrush along the path the wood-witch had taken when she disappeared. He had no idea if he was even going in the right direction. He had to trust his horse to find the way back to its stablemates. Newt had taught him that trick— horses would find water and other horses better than any human could ever hope to.

So he wrapped his arms around the horse's neck, and prayed to the sound of hoofbeats on dirt.

"Gerard!"

It was Tom, Sir Matthias's squire, catching at Gerard's stirrup. He reached for the reins and pulled the horse around, stopping it from running into camp.

"Gerard, where have you been? Sir Matthias—"

"Where is he? Sir Matthias?"

"Gone. Gone to parlay with the local lord, to resupply us in the king's name. He wanted you with him, but no one could find you. Gerard, what's wrong?"

Gerard heard the words, but his brain was already racing ahead. Sir Matthias was too far away now to do any good in time.

Swinging down from his horse, he grabbed Tom by the shoulder. "Walk him until he's cool, then give him grain and water. And find me another horse, plus two more—any that are ready to be saddled right away."

"But—"

"Do it!" Gerard ordered, and Tom, startled by the tone of his command, made a hasty, instinctive bow better suited for a knight than to another squire. Gerard didn't even notice, as he was already striding off in the direction of Newt's bedroll. Without Sir Matthias there, he had only one option; there were only two people who could help. If they weren't there, then he'd look elsewhere.

But there they were: Ailis and Newt sitting on a log, and Callum was perched on the stump the log had come from. Gerard had hoped to do this without an audience, but found himself without a choice.

He cleared his throat and got their attention.

"Gerard!" Ailis jumped up off the log, her hand tugging at her braid in way that always signified unease—or being caught doing something she thought she might get in trouble for. She looked up at him, concerned. "Where have you been?"

Newt, who had been sitting beside her, was slower to stand, his sharp eyes taking in the cuts and scrapes on Gerard's face, and the leaves and twigs that were stuck to his boots and in his jerkin. "Gerard, you look like twenty monsters were after you. What's happened now?"

"Ailis, I need you. Newt, you too, I think. right now!"

"We were—" Ailis started to protest.

"Whatever it was, it can wait. *They* can't."

"Someone's in trouble?" Newt was ready and asking questions. "Where? Who?" Newt might not be a squire, but he understood priorities. Maybe that was why they were friends, despite all the differences between them.

"Come with me," Gerard said.

Callum stood and looked at Gerard. "And me?"

His face was alight with the possibility of going on an adventure with his new friends.

Gerard shook his head. "Not this time." He tried to be considerate, but there wasn't time and he had little experience with this sort of thing. He tried to think what Sir Lancelot—the kindest, gentlest man he knew—might say. "Next adventure, maybe. When I have time to—"

Gerard caught a glare from Ailis and changed his words mid-sentence. "Until we have time to . . . work things out. But not now. We have to move fast, and taking on another person would slow us down."

Callum started to protest. Newt put a hand on his shoulder and nodded his reluctant agreement. The squire was deflated but didn't argue.

"Poor Callum," Ailis said as they walked away, and both boys looked at her as though she had grown a second head.

"I just . . ." She started to explain, then shrugged in frustration. "It's tough to be left out," she said. "Even if you're being left out of stuff that would get you in trouble. You *are* about to get us into trouble, aren't you?"

The horses were penned on the other side of the encampment, near the small creek. Sir Matthias did not outwardly believe any of the stories circulated about the forest, but everyone knew that running water could stop a curse or a witch from crossing, so it made sense to keep the most vulnerable members of his troop there. If nothing more, it made those who were superstitious feel better. Gerard led them around the outskirts of the encampment, keeping close to the trees. As they went, he told them what he had encountered.

"And you think I can do . . . what?" Newt asked. "Ailis, all right, she has her magic. But me? Unless you think my dog-training and horse-grooming skills are going to work on spiders, which, I'm telling you, they don't—"

"I don't know," Gerard admitted. "I'm running on instinct here. And my instinct tells me you need to come along."

"Do you think—" Ailis stopped. "Did you hear that?"

"Hear what?" Gerard didn't even slow down.

Newt paused, looking around carefully, but when nothing popped out of the tree line or came at them from the clearing, he shrugged and moved on briskly.

Ailis waited another moment, her shoulders

hunched as though expecting a blow. "What are you?" she asked, softly. "*Where* are you?"

"Ailis!" Newt was calling back, impatiently waiting for her. Gerard had gone ahead and was now out of sight. Getting the horses, she supposed.

"I know you're there," she said to whatever had made the noise. "So you might as well just show yourself."

When nothing responded, not even the wind, she shrugged and walked on.

"How do you expect to find your way back?" Newt asked Gerard as they left camp, walking the horses as though cooling them down after a ride, so as not to risk anyone asking questions about where they were going.

Gerard was still following his instinct, which was that Ailis and Newt would be what was needed, not a score of overeager warriors. It might merely be wishful thinking, a desire to go back to the simplicity of their former lives, but he didn't think so.

"I left a trail as I rode," he said, pointing to the scraps of cloth on the forest's floor. He had torn off random bits of his shirt and dropped them as he rode. "The forest might be able to open and close at will— or at someone else's will. But I thought it might not be able to find, or move, something of mine."

"Huh? Not bad," Newt said grudgingly, all the more so for the approving glance Ailis sent to Gerard.

The ride was less difficult than Gerard remembered, as though the forest didn't mind him coming back. That unnerved him until he caught Ailis making an open-and-shut motion with her hands, and saw that her mouth was moving. She seemed to be forming silent words that compelled the plant life to back off, just a little.

"See?" he said to Newt, indicating her actions. "Magic can be useful."

"So long as Sir Matthias isn't here to see it, you mean." Newt's voice was scornful.

Gerard blushed angrily at the realization that Ailis had clearly been sharing confidences with Newt. It stung.

The stable boy moved his horse closer to Ailis, bending slightly so that he could speak to her in a low tone. "Is whatever it was still following us?"

Ailis nodded, not breaking her chant.

"I'm going to drop back and see if I can spot it," Newt said, then swung down from his saddle without halting his horse and handed the reins over to

Gerard, who tied them to his own saddle without comment.

When he was a child, before his mother died and he went to live full-time with the dogs in the kennel, Newt used to play hunter-in-the-green, stalking small animals until he could get close enough to touch them. Working with dogs taught him a different style of hunting, but he never let those early skills fade entirely.

If Ailis felt something following them, something was following them. A tension built inside Newt. This skulking, silent thing . . . He *would* find out what it was.

"*Eeeeesssssshhhhhhhh.*"

The sound came from behind him. Newt turned, still moving slowly, expecting to see something. But there was only the twisting of leaves that he reasoned to be the track of something passing—or it might have been a breeze, a fox, or an innocent bird. Not everything in the forest was suspicious. In fact, very little he had seen so far was out of the ordinary, for all the stories surrounding it.

"*Eeeeesssssshhhhhhhh.*" Then there was silence.

Letting out a sigh, Newt moved on as quietly as was humanly possible under the branches, just behind and to the left of the three horses ahead of him. The sense that there was something watching him kicked in again, just a prickle between his shoulders. The more he tried to ignore it, the more it grew, until Newt was almost crying with the need to reach behind him and strike out at something, anything, to make the feeling end.

"Oh, dear God," he heard Ailis cry from up ahead, and gratefully abandoned his fruitless hunt in order to rejoin his friends.

They had slipped out of their saddles as well, leaving the horses hobbled near a large rock. Lying on the ground, nearly concealed by the grass, Ailis and Gerard were staring down at the village where Gerard had left the knights.

They were still there, exactly as he had described. But their armor and jerkins were gone, and the four men were down to their smallclothes and boots, shivering under the spider-spun bonds.

"Their clothing, the armor . . . it's dissolving?" Ailis asked in a hushed whisper.

"Poison," Newt said in a grim tone. "It's something caustic, like lye, to burn off the shell of something they want . . . to eat." He finished his sentence slowly, reluctantly.

"Thanks for telling us that," Gerard said sarcastically. "So, was there anything actually following us?"

Newt wasn't offended by the squire's tone, for once; he wouldn't have wanted to know that, either. "Yes, I'm pretty sure there was. But it's not showing itself. And we have other concerns right now."

The spider-things were fewer in number than Gerard had said, but that made sense, if they had been eating each other.

"They're larger now, too," Gerard said.

"The knights are awake," Ailis said. "Their eyes are all open." Even Sir Brand, whose head was lifted just enough that he could watch the spiders nearest to him.

"The poison might be wearing off," Gerard suggested, trying to figure out how quickly they could cover the ground between them and the knights.

"Our men still can't move, not with those things around them. We'll be easy prey if we try to lug them out." It was almost as though Newt knew what Gerard was thinking. The tension inside him had never really died down. It wasn't a pleasant feeling, making his skin feel tight around his body, but it took his mind off everything else, so he focused on it, trying to feel the extent of it from the skin on down into flesh and bone.

Ailis shifted, and a rock, dislodged by the motion, rattled down the hill. None of the spider-things seemed to notice, but Sir Ruden's head moved, slowly, in their direction. It was too far away to be certain, but his face seemed to have expressed a weary kind of relief.

"You said that the things didn't leave the village?" Newt asked.

Gerard nodded. "They waited until the first knight rode into the village, then they came out of hiding."

"Like they were waiting?" Ailis asked nervously.

"Like they were under orders," he responded.

"A pack. A trained pack, without the ability to do anything on their own?" Newt was in his element here. "Right. We need a distraction, something to drive those creatures away, and give us a chance to rescue the knights."

"We need magic," Ailis said. "*Real* magic."

"Can you do it?" Newt asked her.

Ailis's gaze met his and didn't let go. "I can do it."

* * *

"Wait, wait!" Gerard was speaking to himself as much as to Newt, so the stable boy didn't take the bossiness badly. He, too, knew the moment wasn't right.

Ailis hadn't done anything yet. They had left her by the rock, working through her limited collection of spells and trying to find something that would do the job. The young men had crept on their bellies like snakes until they were as close as they dared to go.

"Wait . . ."

"I know," Newt hissed.

Newt was finding it difficult to keep his attention on the knights. It wasn't Ailis that was distracting him, either; he believed that she knew what she was doing, and watching her wasn't going to make things happen faster. Something else began to twitch at the back of his neck—and the something was probably the thing he and Ailis had felt earlier. Something was still lurking, watching them.

Newt was used to being watched. The dogs he cared for used to watch him slavishly, waiting for a sign, a command, a hint of food. The horses he helped train and groom watched him for continued assurance that they were safe. This was different. It was not like having Merlin watch him, or Ailis, or even

Sir Matthias, the few times he'd come under the knight's eye. It was curious and intense.

Ailis finally caught his eye; she was unbraiding her hair, running her fingers through the thick red strands, letting the wavy mass fall in front of her face and obscure her from sight.

The strands started to move, gently at first, then more wildly, as though a heavy wind had come up, causing her hair to fly all around her head. But around them, the air was entirely still. Her hands raised up and parted her hair so that she could see what was happening. Her face was alight. Her grim smile made it appear as though she was enjoying this—all the danger, all the risk.

Newt had long suspected all users of magic were crazy. This confirmed it. Even sensible, practical Ailis fell victim to it, to the point where she was willing to defy Sir Matthias in order to do more, perform larger, more aggressive spells.

That had been what they were discussing when Gerard found them. Ailis had actually been ranting, and not really talking. And while he agreed with her on most points—especially when she complained about Gerard acting as though he was older, wiser, and better than everyone else—Newt couldn't let go of his own discomfort when it came to her using magic, or anyone using magic. He didn't believe it was wrong or unholy, the way Matthias seemed to think. Newt was just afraid of what—and who—might be getting their hooks into Ailis through that magic.

Newt just didn't trust magic . . . at all.

But he did trust Ailis. Usually.

She raised her face to the sky and began speaking more loudly, but the sound barely carried to where the boys were hidden.

"Time to get moving," Newt said, elbowing Gerard, who merely nodded.

A powerful breeze suddenly rose, blasting out of the trees behind them and rushing down into the village, then swerving suddenly and rushing back up to where Ailis was now standing. She was rock-steady, even in the winds, her arms outstretched to direct where the air should go. Her hair blew madly about her face, keeping clear of her eyes and mouth so that she could continue working the spell, but it wound around her neck and shoulders like live snakes.

She *looked* like a sorceress.

The spider-things, at first oblivious to the magic,

started jittering nervously when the first wave of Ailis's conjured air hit them. Then, like hunters scenting blood, they turned almost as one and started up the hill.

"If they rush her, all at once . . ."

"Don't think," Gerard said. "*Move!*"

As stealthily as they could, the two boys moved across the line of demarcation and into the village. There was a moment of quiet and then, while the little black creatures remained fixated on Ailis, and nothing new rose from the discarded dogs' bodies to challenge them, they raced to the nearest knight.

It happened to be Sir Brand. He was conscious, but barely, and in no shape to even try to break free of the bonds. Newt slung him over one shoulder, staggering a little under the weight, and started back out of the village.

Behind him, Gerard grabbed Sir Daffyd, planning to do the same thing. His hand made contact with one of the white bonds, and he jerked it away, disgusted by the cold, sticky feel of the webbing. Something made him look up then, just in time to see a handful of the spider-things finally turn and head in his direction. His touching the web must have somehow alerted them.

Uh-oh, he thought, then started to lift Daffyd, planning to make a run for it.

"Teine!" Ailis called in a strange language, one hand pointing directly at Gerard. *"Teine!"*

The wind curled around Gerard, shoving him uphill. Then it seemed to thicken, and it heated to an almost unbearable level until sparks flew and a burst of flame erupted from the gust, scorching one of the spider-things, and driving the others back in a skitter of legs and bodies.

It gave him only a few breaths of safety, but he used them, making a mad dash, running faster than he ever thought he could move. He stopped only when Newt reached up and grabbed him, pulling the squire and his knightly bundle down to the ground.

"We have to go back for the others . . ." Gerard was already twisting his body around to get up on his feet again when Newt's hand on his shoulder held him back.

"Let Ailis do her thing first," Newt suggested. "And we need to see if we can get these ropes off them."

"You do that—I have to try and get them out of there!"

Newt swore under his breath, then turned to Sir

Brand. He placed his hands on the spider silk, curled his fingers around the strands and tugged. Behind him, the winds of fire Ailis was directing seemed to falter, but then surged again. The spider-things dodged out of the way. Her lack of control was evident in the near misses, but she was still able to keep them from trying to attack her directly.

"Come on!" Newt muttered, pulling on the threads. He could feel his frustration and anger rising, and tried in vain to ignore it.

"Break already!" he commanded the threads. He closed his eyes and put all his strength into the muscles that years of working in the kennels and stables had given him. He might never swing a sword the way Gerard did, but he knew ropes, and he knew how to break them.

His teeth gritted, he gave one last pull, and the spider-silk strands warmed almost unbearably under the friction of his palm. It frayed and snapped and finally splintered apart.

Thrown onto his backside, Newt blinked up at the sky, then realized that Sir Brand was moving, the rest of the bonds falling loose as the one strand parted. He didn't wait to see how the knight was doing beyond that, but immediately got back up on his knees and moved over to Sir Daffyd.

Time seemed to speed up and slow down all at once, so that Newt felt like he was moving very quickly while everything around him was moving as though underwater, or caught in thick mud. He had finished with Daffyd's bonds and turned back to see if Brand needed any more help by the time Gerard returned with Sir Thomas.

"Ailis . . ."

"Still holding them off," Gerard said. There was an ugly green-and-black mess on his pants leg. Newt decided not to ask about it.

"I'll get Sir Ruden, and we're done," the squire said, before scrambling back into the village. Brand made a move as though he wished to go with him, then his knees gave way and he sat down hard.

"Sir, you might want to rest a bit," Newt said, already too busy to worry about offending the knight. Some of them were on their dignity about the slightest thing, especially if they felt they had been made to look foolish in front of a servant. Fortunately, either Sir Brand wasn't one of those men, or he was too thankful and sore to argue the point. He stayed where he was, watching Gerard go back to Sir Ruden and start to drag him back.

"Who is *she?*" Sir Brand asked suddenly. "The serving girl?" His voice was incredulous.

Newt looked up in time to see Ailis drop down beside them.

"I'm done," she said. Her hair was dripping with sweat, and there was a bruise on the side of her face, as though something had smacked her. Her eyes were exhausted as well, but there was an oddly calm look to her face.

"Any trouble?"

Newt tried to keep his voice nonchalant, not sure how much she would want to admit to having done. Ailis shrugged, clearly aware of the three knights around them. Being cautious, she replied, "I did what had to be done." Newt looked carefully at her, hearing something odd in her voice.

"Girl, you should not be here." Sir Brand's expression changed mid-sentence, from dismay to surprise. "You shot the flaming arrows that distracted the . . . those things?"

"I . . . yes." Ailis was still surprisingly subdued. Even if she was finally learning the wisdom of caution, it was so unlike her usual reaction to using magic— especially such an impressive and successful spell— that Newt's level of concern rose. Before he could press

Ailis for details, Gerard came back with Ruden, and Ailis moved to take care of his bonds. She used her body to block what she did from the other knights. Whatever it was, it took far less time than Newt's attempts, because Sir Ruden shook off the strands a breath later.

"What *were* those things?" he asked, looking to Gerard for answers.

Newt was just as happy to let the squire take the brunt of the knights' attention, because he had just noticed that something was moving under the back of Ailis's tunic, half-covered by her hair—something that had a long, narrow tail which was sticking out from under the bottom of her tunic. He opened his mouth to say something, then closed his jaw quietly. If Ailis wasn't screaming about it, it was clearly something else she didn't want brought to the knights' attention.

"Ah," Gerard said. "You see . . . I went back to camp and sent a message to Sir Matthias, but then I ran into Newt, and we came back directly to lay a better track for Sir Matthias when he came. He saw the spiders simply sitting, as though they were waiting, and . . ."

The knights were all standing up, testing their

legs, trying to get feeling back in their limbs once again, while Gerard attempted to explain himself without actually saying anything that might get them in trouble.

"And you thought that they, like normal spiders, might be afraid of fire? Well done, lad," Sir Ruden said in approval. "Although next time you might consider letting a squire handle the arrows instead of the girl. You wouldn't want one of us to end up burned to a cinder, rather than the beasts."

"Sir, let us give you our horses," Newt offered, afraid that the implied insult to Ailis might make her lose her temper, despite—or perhaps because of—the strange peaceful aura that had settled over her. That tail was still making him uneasy, even if Ailis didn't seem to mind it. "So you can return to Sir Matthias and update him properly on what has happened."

"Yes, a wise thing. You three will be safe walking back?"

"We will be fine," Ailis said hastily. "Gerard is here to protect us from danger, after all." Only Gerard and Newt heard—or understood—the irony in her voice.

It was at that point that Sir Brand suddenly realized that he was standing in front of a girl—a young woman—wearing nothing but his smallclothes and boots. He blushed a deep red. The nearly full-body underclothes worn under mail was designed to keep the metal from touching skin—but it was clearly the situation itself, not the actual exposure, that was embarrassing him.

The horses were collected and handed over, stirrups adjusted for the longer legs of the knights, and the squabbling began over who would be forced to ride double, as there were four of them and only three beasts.

Doing his best to ignore their unknightly behavior, Gerard handed Sir Ruden a small cloth package. From the singed smell that arose from it, and the careful way he handled it, Newt guessed that one of the spider-things was inside. Hopefully very, very dead.

"This should be sent on to Merlin," Gerard said, trying to sound as though he was not giving the older man an order. "He needs to see it."

"You think it was the sorceress?" Very few people said her name, as though afraid it would bring her down on them, but Sir Daffyd went so far as to break off his argument with Thomas in order to cross himself even against the reference.

"If not her, another evil force. Either way, Merlin needs to know."

"You mean, the king needs to know," Sir Thomas said. Gerard shrugged and nodded in the same gesture, suggesting that Merlin and Arthur were one and the same, to his way of thinking. Or that—as Newt suspected—Arthur trusted Merlin to tell him what he needed to know, and save the interesting but not essential details for a less urgent time.

The knights, having finally settled their argument with a coin toss, mounted and went on their way, leaving the three youths behind, suddenly aware that the village to their backs was beginning to smell unpleasantly ripe.

"We should do something about the bodies," Gerard said. They looked at each other, and turned to face the village. There were not only the dogs they had noticed earlier, but also decomposing human bodies—the villagers slaughtered in the first appearance of the spiders.

"Can you take care of it?" Newt asked Ailis.

"Yes," she said, without hesitation. "Are you sure we should?"

"You can't leave bodies just lying out there," Newt said, practical to the end. "Not humans, not dogs, not the horses. It would bring predators, at best. Plague, at worst. Do it."

Ailis looked to Gerard, who nodded his agreement and put a reassuring hand on her shoulder. "This is something Sir Matthias would approve of, I think."

"Oh, do I *care* what he thinks?" Ailis muttered. She raised her hands again, and this time the heated wind was immediate, forming out of her palms and swirling like smoke.

"To the still and chilling bodies below, go!"

Fire leapt from her hands, two high-arcing fireballs that split into multiple projectiles over the town, and fell directly into the dead bodies. The ones they could see burst into contained flames that burned blue-white and died out in a scatter of ash.

"When it's my turn to die, I want to go out that way," Newt told her. "Just so you know."

"Don't push it," she said grimly. "Or I might be tempted to make it earlier than you planned." She was exhausted, and had just a glimmer of her usual sense of humor left, after what she had seen and done.

Gerard was about to say something, when he yelped an embarrassingly high-pitched noise.

"What's that?"

Newt had, somehow, forgotten about the thing on Ailis's back. It had crawled out from under her shift and poked a squared-off snout over her shoulder and through the tangles of her hair.

"Oh. I think that's what was following us," Ailis said. "It seemed really interested in my magic."

She reached back over her shoulder and coaxed the thing out into plain sight. It was a lizard of some sort, almost an arm span long, with black eyes bulging slightly from the side of its flat, rounded head, a narrow but muscular body running into a long tail, and four short, muscled legs with round, webbed feet underneath. Its skin was a mottled green, with two dark red stripes running down its back. It glistened slightly, as though it were covered in sweat, but Ailis handled it calmly, without revulsion.

"What is it?" Gerard seemed taken aback, but Newt, predictably, was curious. If it was a creature of any sort, Newt was fascinated.

He raised a hand, prepared for it to back away or hiss, or exhibit any of the usual reactions wild animals might have to a stranger, but instead the creature raised itself up to meet his touch, pressing the flat top of its head against Newt's palm like a dog anticipating its master's touch.

The skin was cool, drier than he expected, almost like one of the parchments from Merlin's study. Newt could feel an odd thrum through it, as though the creature were purring with satisfaction.

"What is it?" Gerard asked a second time, trying to get a better look. The thing moved gracefully off of Ailis's shoulder and up onto Newt's arm, staring back at Gerard with an unhurried, not at all frightened stare.

"I don't know," Newt said, oddly unsettled by the way the thing had taken to him, "but it seems to like me."

"More than it does me," Ailis noted, pointing to the way its tail was now curling around Newt's arm, as though to brace itself, or indicate a connection of some sort. It ducked its head down to Newt's sleeve, and a narrow pink tongue came out and touched the skin of his hand. Satisfied with whatever it tasted, the lizard climbed farther up his arm, sliding around his neck and nesting as best it could in his collar.

"Whatever it is, I think you've got a new pet," Gerard said.

"Very funny." Newt squirmed a little at the unexpected weight, but decided to leave it be.

They packed up what few belongings they had, and set off to follow the knights back to the encampment.

"So where do you think it came from?" Gerard asked. "You think that's what you felt watching us? Why?"

"I have no idea," Ailis said. "It doesn't seem to be particularly intelligent—"

"Hey," Newt protested, already oddly possessive of the beastie.

"I'm sorry, Newt, but it doesn't."

"Smarter than some knights," Newt muttered, reaching up to stroke the lizard's head. The purr increased slightly in vibration.

"It was attracted to my making the fire," she said thoughtfully, taking Gerard's lead in ignoring Newt's comment. "I think it was cold."

"Not from around here then, is it?" Gerard joked. It was a relatively warm day, now that the sun had fully risen, and they were all sweating more than a little from their exertions.

"It's *definitely* not from around here," Newt agreed, feeling it tickle against his skin. "I think—it's too big to be any kind of lizard I've ever seen before, and I don't recognize the markings, but I think that it might be some kind of salamander."

"A what?" Gerard asked.

"A salamander."

Ailis began to giggle. "You mean it's a *newt*, Newt?"

"Very funny." He scowled.

"It is, actually," Gerard said, grinning.

Newt managed to hold his expression for a few strides, then even he had to see the joke in it. They all crossed out of the trees and back into camp, laughing.

Several of the men from the Quest who were in the act of taking down tarps and chopping firewood stopped to stare at them. On foot, with dirt ground into their clothing and Ailis's hair still loose and windblown, their laughter must have added to an already odd sight indeed. That realization just made them laugh harder. Or perhaps it was just the recognition that they had, once again, saved the day, and there was nobody they could brag to about it. After a while, it really did start to become funny.

"Gerard!" Sir Matthias's bellow could be heard all the way back in Camelot.

"Go," Ailis said, wiping tears of laughter from her eyes and waving the squire on. "He'll want to know what really happened. All of it, Gerard. Don't try to muddy the details, you'll only make things worse for all of us. Go on. We'll catch up with you later."

Gerard raised a hand in farewell and acknowledgment, then turned, dashed past another squire leading two half-saddled horses, and disappeared into the crowd.

"Looks like we're packing up and heading out," Newt said, looking around. "So much for the Shadows being the end of the trail."

"Did you really think it would be? That it would be that easy?"

Newt shrugged, feeling the weight of the salamander on his neck, like an oddly heavy scarf. "I don't think we're going to find it at all," he said. "Not any of the knights, no matter how or where they look, or how pure they are or anything else. I don't think it even exists."

He took in Ailis's expression of disbelief and outrage, and amended his comment. "I think it *did* exist once, yes. But now, after how many hundreds of years? Even if it was kept in the finest reliquary, in the safest location, wood rots and metals are melted down, and anything jeweled might be stolen or sold to buy food in the winter. Holiness doesn't stop you from starving if the crops fail."

Ailis couldn't find anything to say in response to that, and so they walked the rest of the short distance through the encampment in silence.

SIX

Tom had taken down most of Sir Matthias's belongings and packed them for travel by the time they got there, so there wasn't anything for Ailis and Newt to do but collect their own small bedrolls and wait for Gerard to fill them in on what was going on.

"*There* you are!" Callum said, catching his breath.

Ailis sighed, and Newt made a face, but they both turned to greet Callum with reasonably pleasant expressions.

"You're back! What happened?" The young squire was flushed, his arms waving madly in his excitement. "Four of the knights came riding into camp—almost naked—and they didn't want to talk to anyone. They just went straight to where Sir Matthias was, and then they all disappeared into the big tent, and nobody's saying anything!" Callum stopped to take a breath. "Where's Gerard? Sir Matthias was yelling for him something fierce!"

"Ger went to find Sir Matthias," Ailis said. "What's being said in camp?" The first thing you learned as a servant—the thing that Gerard never quite allowed himself to accept—was that gossip was often the best, most accurate way to get news, rather than waiting around for someone official to tell you the story.

And sometimes it was wildly wrong, like the stories about the ghost of the old Roman soldiers who walked the banks of the river, or Sir Lancelot's secret marriage, but after a while you started to learn how to filter out the more outrageous exaggerations.

"People are saying everything. And nothing. The knights encountered Morgain herself, and defeated her. That the Grail came to them in a dream, the way it did to Arthur, and led them into battle. That the knights were distracted, led astray by a beautiful maiden, and had to sell portions of their soul to return to us, and Sir Matthias is going to send them back to the monastery to pay penance and see if their souls can be made whole again."

Callum clearly liked that last story the best. Ailis

bit the inside of her cheek to keep from laughing, and Newt merely shook his head. "We should wait until Gerard comes back," was all he said.

If Sir Matthias was releasing the story, then there was no reason for them to be silent. If he was keeping things close, they would likely need to respect his decision.

"Is anyone else hungry? Because I could eat an entire side of deer by myself," said Newt, changing the subject. They had set off early. Midday had come and gone while they were rescuing the knights, so the moment Newt mentioned food, Ailis's stomach gave off a distinctly indelicate rumble of hunger.

"I know where you can get something to eat," Callum said eagerly, and Newt made a "lead on, then" gesture.

It turned out that many who were waiting for news were gathering near a central fire pit, as much for company as warmth. There were maybe half a dozen knights and their squires, plus a handful of lean and muscled hounds, begging for scraps. Someone was cooking a small pot of a concoction that smelled surprisingly good over the fire. Ailis went over to cadge two bowls and a chunk of bread from the person stirring the pot.

Newt sat down on the ground, claiming a space for the two of them, while Callum, who had eaten already while waiting for them to return, stopped to speak to another squire he knew. *Acquiring more outrageous stories*, Newt presumed.

The salamander slid gracefully down Newt's arm, and marched on its four short legs over to the saddlebag planted at his feet. It crawled in, turned around somehow in the crowded space, and stuck its blunt snout out of the pack, its eyes closed with what could only be described as a blissful expression on its lizard-like face.

Newt, mindful of how cold it had been earlier, picked up the saddlebag and moved it closer, sharing his own body warmth with his newfound pet. A muted purring noise arose from the somnolent creature, as though in thanks.

He had no idea why the creature had decided to adopt him, jokes about his name aside, but it *was* cute, in a sort of slithery fashion, and he certainly wasn't going to abandon it now. Nobody around them seemed to notice the addition to their party, much less object—not even the dogs. And that was very, very odd.

"Here." Ailis handed him a bowl made of

hollowed-out bread, and filled with some kind of damp meat and wilted greens. It smelled much better than it looked, and it tasted slightly better than chewing shoe leather. Newt took a bite, grimaced, and kept chewing. The salamander stuck its head out, sniffed the air, then retreated, unimpressed.

"Got any more of that?" Gerard came over and dropped down on the ground next to them. He had brushed off most of the dirt, and combed his hair, but still looked like he'd spent the morning rolling in the bushes.

"Get your own," Newt said, leaning away in case the squire decided to make a grab for his bowl. It was bad, but it was food, and food he hadn't had to cook.

"Some friend," Gerard muttered, but when Ailis likewise held her food away from him, he got back up with an obvious effort, and went to beg his own bowl.

By the time he came back, Callum had rejoined them as well. There was a momentary standoff, then Callum relented and let Gerard take the better placement on the ground, withdrawing a pace so that, while still obviously sitting with them, he was no longer in the direct triangle of conversation.

"We're moving as soon as all the horses are packed up," Gerard said, swallowing his first mouthful of stew.

"We gathered that much," Newt said, gesturing at everyone with their parcels packed and horses readied. "Because of the attack?"

"Yes." Gerard nodded. "Sir Matthias thinks the entire prophecy was a setup. Half the knights want to go back to the monastery and burn it to the ground, thinking that the monks were agents of Morgain. Sir Matthias had to threaten one of them with a horsewhipping if he even pointed his horse in that direction."

"He thinks it was Morgain who cast the trap?"

Gerard looked at Newt as though the other boy had gone completely mad for even questioning that.

"I'm just asking," Newt said, defensively. "There's no proof. I mean, it's not as though she was standing there, spell in one hand, spider in the other. . . ."

"Spider?" Callum asked, perking up. The other three ignored him. Sir Matthias was telling his men, so the entire story would be over the camp soon enough. It was a matter of pride, now, to be the first to figure out Morgain's intentions. After all, they felt that they did know her best.

"It has her scent on it," Ailis said, surprising them both with the admission. "She likes to use tools to do her work for her, and not to have to come out directly. And we already know that she wants the Quest disrupted."

"And in a way, that will embarrass Arthur as much as possible," Gerard added. "Leaving his knights near-naked and bound by creatures the size of their hands? That would please her."

"I can't imagine the knights telling anyone about that bit," Newt said. "I suppose that would explain the wild stories that are circulating."

Gerard shrugged. "I gave a full report to Sir Matthias. He will give a full report to the king. What happened will be known."

"That's not going to make you too popular," Ailis said.

"Oh, the knights in question have already convinced themselves that they were the ones who managed to turn the tide, using us as a distraction." Gerard's tone was dry, but the way he bent over his meal to hide his face told another story. Yet another chance of glory for him was gone.

"I'm sorry," Ailis said.

"No, it's all right," Gerard said. "It keeps you out of trouble, on the magic front." To this, Callum perked up again, but this time didn't say anything that might interrupt the flow of information. "And, well, they *really* wouldn't have wanted to admit to being rescued by a squire, a stable boy, and a serving girl. They're already cranky enough as it is. Sir Matthias is worried that a number of them might try to abandon the Quest if something doesn't change soon."

"Can they do that?" It was too much for Callum to bear silently. "Didn't Arthur . . ."

Gerard was more patient with the boy than he had been previously. "Arthur picked the knights out of all the volunteers. He didn't order them to go— how could he? It doesn't work that way."

"So she shames them, makes them abandon the Quest, and Arthur's hold on his men is seen as weakened . . . and that makes others think that maybe he's not fit to be king?" Ailis was thinking out loud, putting the pieces together.

"It fits with everything else we know, doesn't it?" Gerard said bitterly. "About what Morgain wants?"

"Do you think she has anything to do with the dissension among the knights?" Gerard went on,

almost hopefully. He would love for all the unpleas-
antness he was seeing among men he respected and
emulated to be caused by evil magic.

"No, I think they're capable of doing that all on
their own," Ailis retorted. Then, seeing how
depressed that thought made him, she added:
"They're just people. I used to clean their rooms.
Trust me, there's not a saint among them. Especially
the ones who try to claim they are."

"What about the salamander?" Newt asked,
diverting the conversation before Gerard became
more melancholy, or Callum's brain exploded with
what they were saying. He was already reluctant to
think badly of his new pet, but reality had to be faced.
"Morgain *does* have a collection of exotic beasts."

All four of them turned to look at the saddlebag,
and saw the salamander was sleeping, oblivious to
the attention.

"He *seems* harmless," Ailis said.

"Is that a magical opinion?" Newt asked.

She shrugged helplessly. "He was certainly
attracted to my working magic, but that might have
been because I was using fire and he was cold. He's
abandoned me quickly enough for Newt, who is
totally non-magical, so . . ."

Gerard turned to Newt and said, "I think . . . Ailis is right. We all agree it's not from around here, but there's no sign it's anything other than just a big newt."

"*Salamander*," Newt corrected him.

"A big salamander. Little newt." Ailis ate the last bite of her bread and wiped her face with her sleeve. "What? It was a joke. Remember those?"

"So I think, unless one of us sees something different, it's not anything we need to tell Sir Matthias about," Gerard said. "Callum, this includes you, too."

Callum swallowed hard, but nodded, clearly thrilled to be involved, even if it was merely to remain silent.

"Or Merlin?" Newt asked.

"We might want to mention it to Merlin, yes. Ailis?"

She shook her head, realizing that her hair was still hanging loose down her back. Her hands now free, she reached back and started to rebraid it as she spoke. "I tried reaching out to him, before I cast the spell, but he was . . . blocked off from me. Not blocked like someone was preventing me from talking to him; I know what that feels like. But more like, 'I'm busy, Ailis, try again later.'"

"You'd think he'd—" Newt broke off, unable to

finish the sentence. Merlin had sent them off on this Quest not only because he believed that they could be useful, but because he thought that Ailis might be somehow contaminated by Morgain's touch—and so in love with magic that she forgot it had a darker side. It was very odd that he would brush her off without knowing what she was trying to contact him about.

"He'd what?" Ailis turned her hazel eyes on Newt, curious.

"He'd have the ability to handle more than one job or thought or conversation at a time," Gerard said. "He certainly managed to yell at us while talking to himself all the time.

"Anyway, it doesn't matter now. I wanted to tell you that Sir Matthias said we did well to burn the bodies—I didn't tell him how we did it—and he is going to request that the monks send someone to say a prayer over the village, maybe pour holy water there or something. It's the least they could do, since one of their own sent us here."

"It would be funny, though, wouldn't it," Ailis said, "if the Grail actually was here in this forest somewhere."

"If it is, it's nowhere we'd be able to find it. Not

unless Newt has a dog somewhere that can sniff out religious objects."

"Monks, yes," Newt said. "Grails, no."

"So where are we going?" Ailis asked. "Or does Sir Matthias just want us out of the Shadows, and doesn't care where we go?"

"He thinks, actually, that the monk's prophecy may have had some truth to it. We were just misdirected. There's an old tower up the coast, maybe two days away, that is reported to throw odd shadows at the wrong time of day, as though something inside it were glowing."

"And that's where we're going? To an unpredictable tower?"

"That's where we're going," Gerard said, shrugging as though to admit that he had no say in the matter.

"That's what I love about this Quest," Newt said to his still-sleeping pet. "All the details we're getting. You really feel the confidence."

"It's not about confidence," Ailis said, as exasperated as he knew she would be.

"It's about *faith*." The boys finished her sentence for her, speaking at the same time. She glared equally at both of them, and glared at Callum, too, in order to make him feel included. Then she flipped her braid back into place and looked up at the sky.

"Merlin? Can I turn them both into chickens? Please? It wouldn't take that much magic, and nobody would notice, really. . . ."

SEVEN

"The best of Camelot," Merlin said in disgust, echoing, unknowingly, Sir Matthias's earlier comment. "May the gods help us all."

The owl he was speaking to turned its head and hooted mournfully at him. The fact that the owl had the same reaction, no matter what he said to it, was less annoying than the fact that the beast was actually stuffed with sawdust, and so had no thoughts at all in its feathered head.

On the other hand, it made for a soothingly placid audience when Merlin felt as though his own head might explode.

He could not blame Sir Matthias for splitting the knights up; he might even have suggested it himself. Small groups were able to move quickly and be less of a burden on the local communities they passed through. . . . It was a good move, a wise move. It was something he would expect a seasoned war leader like Matthias to come up with when faced with stubborn knights and an elusive goal.

Arthur forgot, sometimes, the cost of moving his people from point to point. That was what he had field marshals and stewards for.

Merlin didn't care, actually, about the cost. His job was to get things done. The difference between him and Arthur was how they paid the cost of their decisions. Arthur paid out in gold and royal approval. Merlin paid of himself, in aches and pains and loss of essence.

"I'm far, far too old for this," he muttered, stretching out his legs and feeling them creak. He had discarded his usual robes for more comfortable pantaloons and an exotic billowing tunic. He would never wear them in public, of course, but for intense spell-casting, the wizards of the far-off eastern deserts had the right idea when it came to comfort.

On his worktable, four small vials that represented the king's four groups were set upright, their contents smoking gently, in colors alternating between a thick, smoky gray and flashes of blue, and occasionally spiking into red or green. Red meant he needed to do something, and green meant whatever he had done was working. It was a crude method, but with four bands of knights instead of one to watch, on top of everything else he was being asked to do, crude did the job.

Two of the vials had sparked a violent red this morning, while a third had a slow thread of scarlet rising in its smoke. He had taken the first two and made an additional spell of protection around them, and the men it represented. The third had required more; he had spent almost all morning putting that flame out. By then, the slow thread in the third had turned to a faint pink, and then faded away entirely; whatever crisis was brewing, it had been dealt with on the ground. That had been Sir Matthias's group, he noted.

Merlin rather liked Matthias, even though he was one of those men who worried about the effect of magic on his Christian soul. He wasn't going to find the Grail, not with his particular prejudices and blind sides. The Grail might be holy from its association with the Christ, but it had been touched by many faiths, many beliefs since then, and all had left their mark on it. As was the inevitable way of all living things.

Matthias was a perfect example of that: raised by

a faerie sorceress, taught by a monk, oath-bound to a Christian warlord of pagan descent . . .

It would be an interesting chart to work out, if he didn't already have so much work to do already. First and foremost: Advise and protect Arthur as he deals with the daily business of his kingdom. Never a simple act, but one he knew well. And he had to keep the general protections in place around Camelot. By now, that was something he could and did do in his sleep. But the fact that Morgain had been able to sneak her way in—that had caused him to yank up all his protections by the roots, checking each one for flaws, and then regrounding them more firmly inside the castle walls—a time consuming and energy-draining process.

Merlin was also bound to the task of finding the identity of the shadowy figure the children had reported seeing in Morgain's keep. Arthur and he were in agreement on the fact that Morgain was a threat, but a known one. This new player in the game was disturbing. Anything that shifted the balance of the game they played was to be taken seriously.

Those three things alone were enough to stress even an enchanter such as himself to near breaking. And Merlin also had to protect the knights on their holy Quest for the Grail, without them noticing that they were protected by that dubious figure of an enchanter, naturally.

It was necessary. He had not exaggerated when speaking to the girl-child Ailis: It *was* essential that the Grail come to Arthur, and that the knight who brought it was to keep his eye on the greater glory, not his own enrichment. To do that, Merlin needed to know where they were, and what they were doing at every moment of every day. But he also had to sleep at some point.

"Merlin, do this. Merlin, accomplish that. Merlin, since you're not doing anything, can you balance a sword on the tip of your nose as well?"

Balancing the sword would be easier at this point than trying to keep track of every single knight in each group.

"The things I do for you, Arthur, and your kingdom . . ."

He rubbed the bridge of his nose, trying to ease the strain between his eyes. There were potions he could make for it, of course, but adding that might distract him from something else he had to do. If only he had a proper student to do it for him . . .

"Seafeathers," he cursed. *The girl-child*. She had been trying to reach him again. Was it a day ago? An hour ago? His sense of time, never accurate to begin with, had entirely slipped away since the Quest had begun. No, he had no time to spare for students now. Not if he was to do any of the half-dozen impossible things his king asked of him. But that was no excuse for turning her away if she were in need.

Still. She had reached out, and then gone away. So either the distress had been unimportant, in which case he was not needed, or she had resolved the situation on her own, in which case he was not needed. Or if it was too late now, he was not needed.

There were priorities. And, as dear as the girl-child and her two friends might have become to Merlin the person, Merlin the enchanter had other things he had to attend to first.

"She's a smart girl, Ailis is," he said to the owl. "And the boys with her—they've done well, very well. Toss them into water, they swim. Toss them into the air, they fly. If they need me, they will reach out again."

The owl swiveled its head and looked at him, but did not respond.

"And now for my other problem child," Merlin muttered, turning to a mirror that was propped against a nearby wall.

"Show me my king," he commanded it.

* * *

Arthur was not accustomed to riding out alone anymore. The boy he had been—Wart the orphan boy—had gone everywhere alone, or with just a hound to accompany him. But the High King of Britain went nowhere without a full retinue, a mini-court to watch his every move.

This evening, he had slipped out, using the secret passages of Camelot they all thought he didn't know about, the small tunnels and hidden doors.

He rarely used the secret ways, preferring to keep them for times of great need like tonight.

A decent distance from the walls and the guards stationed therein, Arthur slid down off the nondescript mount he'd taken from the stables and let the beast chomp at the short grass.

"I know you're there," he said calmly.

She did him the courtesy of not dragging things out, respectfully not making a splashy entrance. Morgain merely stepped out of the air as though walking through a doorway.

"Good evening, Morgain. You look well."

"You have something you wanted to say? An offer perhaps? A surrender?"

"Leave my knights alone, Morgain. Leave my people alone."

"Your people?" She raised one eyebrow as though astonished. "Have you marked them, as you do your cattle?"

He sighed, his broad shoulders slumping. "Morgain, I don't want to argue. I never want to argue with you. Why don't you understand that what you ask is impossible? The times you remember are gone, long gone. This is the new way, the way of the future. You need to let go of the past."

She hissed at him, like an angry cat.

"You are my sister; my blood."

"Only half. And you turned from it, Arthur. You turned from the old ways of our mother, and took up the Imperial banner when it landed in the mud where the soldiers of Rome dropped it as they fled this land."

His hand went instinctively to the brooch holding his cloak at one shoulder; an eagle made of silver, its wings outstretched to swoop and strike. "I took what was good of their ways, and what was good of ours, and made something new; something strong. I honor laws made by man. I don't rule by blood and incantation. Camelot is governed by laws everyone can see, can feel, and can appeal to for justice."

His gaze was as impassioned as hers.

She sighed and said, "You are my brother, Arthur. I remember the day you were born. I held you in my arms, wiped your first tears . . . before Merlin took you away." She paused and her normally glorious eyes were filled with an undeniable sadness. "But we have drawn lines and chosen sides. We have nothing more to say to each other."

With that, she turned and disappeared back through the air, leaving Arthur standing there feeling alone.

Back in Camelot, Merlin sighed as he watched his king remount his horse and ride slowly back to the safety of the castle. "Some day you will trust me enough to allow me to arrange these meetings of yours within your own walls, rather than riding out into her clutches," he told the image, ignoring the irony of asking the man he was spying on to trust him. "Some day she is going to try and harm you, and then where will we all be?"

But even as he muttered, he knew it was pointless. Morgain would never harm Arthur directly, not physically. She was, as he had said, his sister. And she loved him, as much as she knew how.

But that would not stop her from doing what she felt needed to be done. And if Arthur could not be equally ruthless, well, it was Merlin's job to do it for him.

EIGHT

"This entire Quest has been cursed from the start." The speaker was striding in a circle around his fellows, gesturing grandly, wildly with his hands. "First, the sleeping sickness Morgain cast upon us all, then the uprising of the border lords, and now this."

"What, rain?" One of the other men, sharpening his dagger with slow, careful strokes against a whetstone, didn't look up from his task as he mocked the speaker. "William, it's *rain*. So you get a bit wet. You're always a bit damp, anyway."

The knight complaining was neither amused nor distracted. "Endless failures! Had I been given *my* choice of whom to follow—"

"You would have chosen to follow Sir Galahad, perhaps? Or Sir Lancelot?" Sir Ruden shook his head. "So would everyone, and the problem would still have remained. Besides," Sir Ruden went on, stretching his legs out in front of him as though still expecting any moment to find them bound in spider silk again, "they haven't found it either yet, have they?"

"They might have," Sir William said sullenly.

"William, by all that's holy, you see plots against you in every move every other soul makes. They would have told us had the Grail been found," the fourth knight in the group said. He was polishing his boots halfheartedly, not even trying to get the worst of the caked-in mud off the heels.

"Hah." Sir William brushed that comment off with a particularly elaborate wave of his arm. "They'd be on their way back to Camelot, bearing their prize before them. They would not bother to send so much as a messenger-bird to tell us—not until they had secured the king's favor once and for all."

"Assuming they bothered to take it to the king at all," Simon, the knight sharpening his dagger, said.

"What?"

"Think of it. The Grail. Power." Simon's eyes brightened. "The power of the thing . . . Are we certain all our fellow knights would bring it back to Arthur, rather than keep it for themselves?"

"Or take it to another master?" William added, warming to the idea.

"None would dare!" Sir Ruden was outraged.

The knife-sharpener shrugged, pragmatic. "Who could stop them? Who would even know to stop them?"

"You will not speak that way about men of the Round Table," Sir Ruden demanded in his northern accent, getting to his feet. "They are your fellow brothers in knighthood, I might add." His squire rolled up the map they'd been studying, smearing the precious inks as he did so, and tried to get out of the way.

"I am indeed their brother, a member of the Round Table, as well, and may speak as I see fit."

"You will not!"

Sir Ruden launched himself at Simon, but kicked Sir William as he did so, perhaps accidentally, but perhaps not. A fifth knight, who had been silent until then, tried to separate the two men, and received a black eye for his efforts, which made him start swinging as well.

Gerard got up from the log he had been perched on, and, as the brawl spread, walked away. This was the worst he had seen it, but in the two days of riding since leaving the Shadows, the tension had grown even worse among the knights. Even the ones like Sir William, who were normally calm and thoughtful, seemed infected by some bee-sting of dissatisfaction. Nothing was good enough, be it the horse they were riding, the food they were eating, or the hue of blue of the sky above them. And when the topic turned to the Grail, as it often did, frustration and anger would fly freely.

Gerard kicked at a rock that happened to get in his way, and wished that he had never heard of the Grail, never dreamed of coming on this Quest. He almost regretted becoming a squire.

"I don't mean that," he said quickly, in case God, or anyone, had been listening to his thoughts. "I don't." He couldn't imagine being anything else, being anywhere else.

"Even men of valor, even men of great deeds, have the flesh and failures of other men."

Merlin had said that, and he even added "and women as well," before Ailis could gloat. This entire trip had shown him the truth of that.

It had also shown him men of valor as well. Sir Ruden, for all that he might be short-tempered and reckless, had dealt well and wisely with the spider-things. Sir Joseph had charged in to save a squire who had gotten too close to a wild boar, at risk to himself and his steed. And back at Camelot, of course, there was Lancelot, and Sir Gawain, and his own master, Sir Rheynold.

But at this rate, he doubted there was anyone in this group who would be allowed anywhere *near* the Grail, himself included.

He wasn't feeling very noble, or valiant, or virtuous today. He had slept poorly, and woken early, only to find Newt and Ailis already awake, washing their extra clothing in a bucket of water by the fire, Newt's red-striped pet lounging nearby.

He had seen them laughing and joking, familiar and comfortable. They had not noticed him.

Once, Gerard and Ailis had been close—the newly arrived page and the orphaned serving girl. Time and new responsibilities had changed that, but they had always been friends. Always.

"You're a squire. You'll be a knight someday, in a few years, maybe. You won't be able to go on adventures with serving girls and stable boys then." Ailis's words, an echo of Sir Matthias's own words, and Sir Rheynold's, too, were a bitter companion.

When they had made camp, after moving out of

the Shadows, Gerard had set his bedroll up near Tom, Sir Matthias's squire, who had an uncanny gift for finding the softest ground anywhere within a campsite. He had thought that the company might be nice, as well. But the other boy was still off running errands, or cleaning tack, or doing any of the endless number of things he was asked to do for Sir Matthias.

Sir Matthias had no need for his special aide tonight. No one, it seemed, had any need for him.

All right, enough of that. He was a noble squire, of the blood of Sir Kay, the king's own foster brother. He was the squire of Sir Rheynold, and temporarily special aide to Sir Matthias, King Arthur's chosen representative for Camelot on this Quest. He had friends and important work, and his name was known by his king, and by the king's enchanter. He did not have a hard life. Self-pity was simply not acceptable.

It was, however, distinctly satisfying sometimes.

Gerard cleared a space, dug out a depression in the dirt, and set a circle of fist-sized stones around the hole. Not very large, just enough to hold a small fire, as much for comfort as warmth.

Once he had a decent blaze going, thanks to a

handful of twigs and a deadfall of logs, Gerard pulled his bedroll over to sit on. Hugging his arms around his knees, he stared into the fire, glumly contemplating everything that hadn't gone right since Arthur first announced the great and glorious Grail Quest.

Something skittered off to his left, and Gerard's hand reached out to grasp the hilt of his sword, placed carefully beside his bedroll.

"Oh. It's only you."

The salamander came up beside his elbow, looking curiously at him, then at the fire, then back at him.

"It's a fire," he said. *And I'm talking to a newt. Nice, Gerard. Real nice. Could your life become any more depressing?* But he was laughing to himself as he thought it.

The salamander gave off its odd chirping noise, then moved closer and rested its head on Gerard's hand like a dog might do.

Gerard, however, felt no inclination whatsoever to pet it. Especially when the thing's tongue came out and flicked at the fire.

"Careful. It'll burn you."

He still wasn't entirely sure about this creature—

where it came from, why it seemed so interested in them.

But if Ailis said it didn't have the scent of Morgain on it, he was willing to leave it alone for now. Gerard thought it might like the way Newt smelled. Or—and Gerard grinned involuntarily— maybe it heard someone speaking to Newt, and thought they were calling *it*.

The salamander slid off his knee and moved closer to the small bonfire, looking back at Gerard, then back at the fire, almost as though asking per- mission.

"What?"

The salamander merely looked at him and then back at the fire.

"You'll burn yourself if you get much closer," Gerard warned it. The salamander did inch closer, until it was only a hand-span away from the now heated stones, and looked back again at the squire, with what might have been yearning in its small black eyes. Gerard just shrugged, feeling too sorry for himself to really care what it did.

"Sure, go ahead, burn yourself up for all I care. Just don't stink too badly while you do it, okay?"

By the time he had finished the sentence, the

salamander had moved with surprising speed into the fire, sliding over the hot rocks like a fish returning to water.

"Hey," Gerard said, tempted to reach out to grab it back. "Um. Hey!" Because far from burning itself to a foul-smelling cinder, the salamander was lying in the middle of the fire, its tail curled contentedly around its body as it basked in the flames.

"That's new and different," Gerard said in disbelief. Then again, after a dragon, a troll, a bridge made of moonlight, and a griffin, to name just a few of the things he had seen recently, perhaps it wasn't so different after all.

"Does Newt know you can do this?"

The salamander merely closed its eyes and hummed in contentment.

"The sad thing is, you're not even the strangest thing I've seen today, much less in my entire life."

The salamander ignored him, so Gerard went back to contemplating the sorry state of his own existence. He had gotten as far as wondering why he had not taken more credit for being the one to defeat Morgain at swordpoint, noting how instrumental he was discovering the key to reversing the sleep-spell and awakening Arthur and his court, when a muffled squeak broke him out of his depressing thoughts.

"Oh. Hello." He really didn't want to see Ailis right now. Especially since she didn't seem at all interested in even looking at him, instead staring past his shoulder at the fire.

Stupid salamander.

"It's not burning," Ailis said in wonder.

"No, I know." Gerard noticed Newt standing behind Ailis, and shrugged. If they were going to go around joined at the hip, they were going to be joined at the hip. "Didn't know your pet could do that, huh?"

"No. It's never done anything like that before. Constans, come out of there!"

"Constans?" Ailis echoed.

They both looked at him askance. Newt shrugged, an odd look on his face. "It seemed to fit."

Ailis shook her head. "So, it just came over and walked calm-as-calm into the fire?"

"No, actually," Gerard said, thinking it over. "It came over and looked at the fire. Then it waited."

"For what?"

Gerard thought for another moment. "For permission," he said finally. After sitting here with the creature, it seemed perfectly natural to him, but the expression on his friends' faces made him stop and shrug. At least Callum wasn't around to hear how foolish he sounded.

"From you?" Newt was incredulous.

"I was the only one here," Gerard pointed out.

"You built the fire?" Ailis asked.

"Yes."

"And it never did that before?" That question was directed at Newt.

Newt was still staring at Constans. "I've only had it a few days. But no."

"It asked permission of the owner of the fire. That's interesting." Ailis was leaning so far over to watch Constans, she was in danger of singeing her hair. Gerard reached out and tugged her arm, pulling her away.

"Wait," she protested. "I want to try something."

She reached out over the fire and tapped one of the flames, muttering something Gerard didn't quite understand under her breath. "Ow!"

"Fire. It burns," Newt said. "So now you know."

"Very funny," she said, turning on him. "I was trying to see—"

"Ailis? Witch-child?"

All three of them yelped, Ailis almost fell into the fire. Newt grabbed her by the arm and hauled her out of the way just in time.

The fire spat cinders. Flickers of deep blues and greens jumped up from the wood.

"Did you hear—?"

"No," Newt said. "I didn't. And you didn't either." He tried to move her away. "Constans, you too, come out of there, now."

The salamander heaved a heavy sigh, but started to emerge from the flames, when suddenly a hand reached out of the fire and held it there.

This time, their yelps were louder.

"Witch-child? Answer me! I can feel you."

"That's not me, that's Constans," Ailis managed to say, despite her shock. "Please let go, you're hurting him."

The hand disappeared, and Constans scurried out of the flame, the red stripes on its back faded to normal as it reached Newt. Hesitant at first, Newt put a finger to the salamander's skin and then, discovering that it was still somehow cool, picked it up and let it slide back under his collar.

Meanwhile, where the hand had been, another image was taking shape in the flames.

It was Morgain, her long black hair framing her pale face, backlit by the flames surrounding her. "Witch-child, I need your help," she said. "All Britain needs your help."

NINE

"You can't be serious. Ailis, didn't we talk about this? Morgain is not to be trusted!"

They had stepped away from the fire, where Morgain's image still flickered, beautiful and impatient. It was Gerard's worst nightmare, in so many ways: Ailis being called back by Morgain and Ailis being tempted.

Newt, too, was feeling the same concern.

"She lies, Ailis," he said to her.

"She has never lied to me. When has she ever lied to you?"

Newt had to think about that. "All right. But she doesn't tell the truth, either. She's using you! Manipulating you, and your desires . . ."

"Who hasn't?" Ailis looked at him, then Gerard. "What adult hasn't said to us, 'If you do that, we can give you this'? Merlin has done nothing *but* manipulate us to his own ends. Arthur, too. We're simply tools to them all. Morgain, at least, offers me the chance to become more than a tool. Merlin? Arthur? Sir Matthias? What have they ever given us besides 'not yet' and 'go do this, as well' as a reward? This Quest, this journey—it isn't a reward. It's just another thing they need for us to do. Do you think I didn't know Merlin wanted to use me as bait here?"

The two boys avoided looking at each other, effectively confirming that they had known.

"You can't lie on the astral plane," Ailis went on. "Not effectively; not if you're not paying full attention to the lie, and Merlin never has his full attention to give to anything.

"But Morgain . . . She's never lied to us. She's been honest, in her own way, with us. Is she the enemy? Yes. But . . . I don't think she always was. I don't think she always has to be." Ailis was remembering things Morgain had said to her while the girl was held hostage in the sorceress's castle. *This is my land. My blood is pure—purer than Arthur's. My family ruled long before the Pendragon came here and raised his flag, and it should have been* mine. *But when my father died . . . Uther the King decided that my mother would be his bride. And there was nothing she could do to stop him. Arthur came of that union. A boy, and because he was a boy, all the power and the glory went to him. Not the girl-children my mother had borne before. Not the ones with the true power, the magic, the Old Ways in their blood.*

"If she says that the land needs us . . . I have to at least listen to what she wants to say."

"We barely escaped last time, Ailis!" Newt protested. "Both times, we barely got away! And you want to step directly into the fire and go back into . . . go back to her? Into her clutches?"

Ailis stood her ground. *"Yes."* She stared Newt in the eye, then relented. "She *needs* us now. *We* have the upper hand."

"She wants us to *think* that we have the upper hand."

They sounded ready to go back and forth all night, so Gerard said the only thing he could think of. "Sir Matthias will never allow it."

"And that is why I'm not going to tell him," Ailis said.

"Ailis!" Gerard couldn't believe what he was hearing. "You cannot just leave the Quest like that!"

"You mean I can't just ride off on the word of a

strange female without telling anyone—least of all Sir Matthias—where I am going or why?"

Gerard's first reaction was to retort, "That was different." He managed to bite back the words before they doomed him to one of her wicked glares, or worse. He didn't *think* that she knew how to turn him into a frog yet . . . but he wasn't willing to risk it.

"Besides," she went on, reassured that neither he nor Newt had any comments to add. "I won't be riding off—Morgain's offered to make a portal . . . and I won't be going entirely without a word. You two will be here to explain."

Ailis turned her back on them and walked back to the fire. "I'm ready," she said.

No sooner were the words out of Ailis's mouth than a ring of flame appeared over the fire, growing in size until it was an Ailis-sized oval rising out of the embers, crackling and snapping silently in the air.

As magic went, it was simple, but no less impressive for it. And without a single glance back, Ailis stepped through and disappeared.

"I don't know about you," Newt said. "But I'm not staying behind to explain this."

In two strides he was at the fire. With a third, he was through.

Gerard hesitated half a breath, then checked to make sure his sword and dagger were firmly attached to his belt, and followed.

He had no sooner gone through than the portal closed, almost on his heels, with a cold whoosh of air followed by an audible *snap*.

In the silence that followed, the small fire flickered once, as though someone had stirred the flames, then died.

* * *

"Ailis?" In the distance, within the cool stone walls of Camelot, Merlin lifted his head from his work, and sniffed the air like a hound scenting a new trail. "Huh." He shook his shaggy head and returned to the complicated spell he was waving, muttering, "I could have sworn I heard her. . . ."

* * *

"All three of you. There's a surprise." The sorceress's tone indicated that it was anything but a surprise to her.

They were in a small room with cream-colored stone walls. The air was cool and still, and off in the distance he thought he could hear the sound of water.

Ocean tides. They were back in her keep, in the Orkneys.

He still didn't like using magic. He didn't trust this kind of travel. But, now that they had learned how to go through without landing in a pile of bodies on the other side, he had to admit there were advantages to it.

"You called us, Morgain. So please talk. Or we're turning around and going right back." Ailis might have been bluffing—once in Morgain's stronghold, anything she tried would be overwhelmed. Only she didn't *sound* like she was bluffing, to Newt's ear. That frightened him almost more than Morgain.

The sorceress didn't seem to take Ailis's words as a threat. From the flicker in her dark eyes, Newt would have sworn that she was pleased. Like a mother cat when a kitten brings home its first mouse.

"Are you certain that you can open a portal here? One that I do not first allow?"

"Are you certain that I need your permission to do anything?" Ailis countered.

There was absolutely obvious satisfaction in Morgain's gaze, Newt was certain of it.

Morgain was dressed somberly in a dark green dress, her hair braided in a crown around her head.

The great black cat they had seen at her feet before kept her company again, sleeping by the stoop of the single door, guarding the exit.

Or was it guarding the entrance? Newt suddenly wondered. Unlike the previous times they had encountered her, Morgain did not seem to be entirely the mistress of her world. Now he could see that there were faint creases around those glorious dark eyes, and her mouth, rather than curving in a mocking smile, was pressed into a narrow line.

"Morgain . . ." Ailis was clearly losing patience.

"I have made an error," Morgain said, clearly having to fight to get the words out. "My life has been . . . I was raised to lead, not follow. I am my father's daughter, as well as my mother's." Her father, Gorlois, had been a warlord of note before he died in battle, riding with Uther, Arthur's father.

"Your point?" Ailis pressed, all but tapping her boot-clad foot in impatience. They had come here for answers; not drama.

"She wanted her share." Gerard didn't come right out and yawn, but he looked ready to do it. "The only threat to Britain, Morgain, has been you. So why are we here again?"

The sorceress's eyes flashed angrily at his words,

with actual sparkles of magic forming in her frustration. "If I had wanted to kill you—if I had wanted to kill Arthur—I would have already."

Gerard bristled in reaction to that, and snapped back, "And you would have found nowhere to hide, had you murdered your brother. Even those who support you—"

"Murdering family members occurred with great regularity in this island's history, as recently as my parents' time," Morgain said, then waved one elegant hand as though to dismiss the threat, bringing the tension in the room back down.

"I had my reasons for what I have done. I still have my reasons. I do not apologize for them."

"Your point, Morgain?" Ailis said again, heading off another explosion of outrage from Gerard.

"I began my current project with the intent to shake Arthur, to make him acknowledge me as his peer, perhaps even as co-regent; certainly as heir."

That was not unheard of, to have a sibling—even a half sibling—take the throne, especially as Arthur had no acknowledged children.

But Newt doubted, quite strongly, that Morgain would ever be accepted within Arthur's court, much less as a potential queen. He knew better than to voice those thoughts, certainly not within her own keep. Morgain might seem subdued and apologetic this instant, but that was to be trusted as much as a fox's smile—not at all.

"My . . . ally promised to enhance my power, to make me stronger, and more able to take on Arthur, to bring him to the parley table."

To bring the king to his knees, all three of them mentally translated. They knew Morgain now. Not one of them believed she was interested in any negotiations she did not control.

"And now?" Ailis asked.

"And now the price of that promise has been revealed in full. It is a price that, upon consideration, I am not willing—not able to pay."

"Reneging on her agreement . . . what a surprise," Gerard said, and got a kick in the shins in response. When he glared at Newt, the other boy made a gesture that told him to keep quiet.

Morgain ignored the boys, focusing on her one-time, would-be student. "Do you remember what I told you, witch-child, about my bloodlines?"

Ailis did. "That you were tied to the land, magically, in order to better care for it and the people living there."

"A simplification, but the heart of the matter, yes. Some of those ties involved rituals, ways we were bound ourselves not only to the earth but the very soul of this island. As our fortunes went, so, too, did the land. And as the land went, so too did we." Her face took on a faraway expression of longing.

"It was no terrible burden, no thing too hard to bear. My bloodline *is* the land, after all. Every handful of soil, every drop of water . . . Even now, this England, this unified-under-Christ England my brother dreams of, my blood is what feeds all these lands. I love it beyond passion. Beyond logic. Beyond my own life. I have no choice." Morgain stared wistfully over Ailis's shoulder.

"My ally . . . does not love this land," Morgain continued. "I did not understand that until last night. Until it was, perhaps, too late. Under the calm it shows the world, there is a seething madness."

She shook her head, then looked at Ailis, the haze that had fallen over her eyes finally clearing.

"It has created a spell, a form of sympathetic magic."

Ailis nodded, indicating that she understood, but the boys looked lost. Morgain explained. "Take a map, for example. Shape it as closely as possible to the actual land it covers. Then burn it, and fires will ravage the land itself."

"It has created such a map?"

"Of Albion, yes."

Albion was the name Morgain used when she was thinking of the Britain of her mothers, before the Romans came; the *magical* Britain, not the one Arthur ruled.

"My ally used my own flesh and blood in the making, claiming that it will allow me to manipulate spells more effectively. All I need to do is activate the latent magic within. But I fear what it truly plans to do with the map, should I touch the spark within my blood and create the spell."

"So don't create the spell," Newt said, all practicality. It seemed straightforward to him.

"If I do not . . ." She paused. "We have gone too far at this point. When I called my companion, it granted certain permissions I may not revoke. The ramifications of doing so, of breaking that agreement, would run back along the lines of magic and destroy me."

"And we care about this?" Gerard sounded as cold-blooded as Newt in this matter. "I'm sorry, Ailis, but seriously. Arthur doesn't want the blood of his sister on anyone's hands, but if she brings it on herself . . ."

"My death will serve the same purpose as if I were to ignite the map myself," Morgain said. "All those years of tying ourselves to the well-being of the land is a dual-edged sword. As the land goes, so does my strength, my power. And the return is true as well."

Gerard looked puzzled as he tried to figure out what she meant. Ailis understood it right away. "If you die . . ."

"Without a child, preferably a girl-child, to carry on the line . . ." Morgain's expression turned cold, like the gray clouds of a storm gathering. "If I die, so, too, does the land, unless a successor has been chosen and marked with the blood and soil of the land; vows made must be witnessed, and sealed."

Gerard started to protest, and Morgain turned her cold face to him. "Did you not understand? In so many ways, I *am* the land. As Arthur could have been—as he feels the urge to be, but he has chosen to rule differently. And he has no child, as yet, to placate the land.

"Without that, without one of my line to offer ourselves in service, to *be* the land—crops will fail, wells will run dry, the hunting and fishing returns will decrease, year after year.

"If my ally manages to drain my power into itself, it will control the rise and fall of our fortunes. This land, under its maddened whim . . . it does not bear thinking of."

"What can we do to stop it?" Ailis asked.

"Against the companion? Nothing. You do not have the power. Only *I* can do that."

"But you said . . ." Gerard protested, shaken by the idea that she had told them all this merely to leave them helpless.

"I said I need your help, that the land needs your help. And we do."

Morgain got up from her chair to pace. The giant cat by the door opened its sleepy green eyes to watch her pass, then went back to sleep.

"In my increasing frustration at Arthur's narrow-mindedness and his failure to take up the old ways, I called this ally to me, at the Well of Bitter Water."

The phrase seemed familiar to Ailis, but she couldn't quite remember why.

"I tied myself to my ally," Morgain went on, "made vows and obligations, as my ally vowed and obligated itself to me in return.

"This is how such magics are worked, witch-child." Even under the circumstances, Morgain was a teacher, willing her students to understand, as well as accept, what she said. Newt began to see a little of what Ailis found so appealing in the woman. "You must give, in order to receive, no matter who or what you are."

"So what can we do?" Newt asked, still not quite understanding their role.

"Help free me from my obligation, so that I may strike out against it, without that strike damaging myself as well. In order to be freed, I must know the source of its power—its true name."

"You called it, and you don't know its name?" Newt was openly dubious.

Morgain shifted her attention to him. It was uncannily like being the focus of Arthur's regard.

Newt felt both comforted and disturbed by that reminder that they two were, after all, half siblings.

"Not what it is called, but its True Name, the name given to it at Creation."

"And that would be . . ." Gerard asked.

Morgain looked at the squire as though he had

just been discovered under a particularly heavy, flat rock.

"If I knew what it was, I would not need your assistance to free myself, would I?"

"Why us? Why not Merlin?"

"Because Merlin's too powerful," Ailis said, finally figuring it out. "She won't indebt herself to him. To us—she can accept that. Anything we ask of her in return, she thinks she can either grant, or find a way out of it."

"And if *we* go to Merlin?"

"Then we're the ones indebted to him, not her."

"Oh. Right." Newt understood how favors worked. "So, what, we're supposed to hare off across the island, without a clue . . ."

Morgain and Ailis both sighed in exasperation. Gerard said, "I never said I did not know where it was hidden, merely that I did not know it," Morgain said. "It watches me too closely, too carefully, for me to go search for it myself.

"Go to its source, the place where I called to it." She withdrew a small, rolled parchment from the sleeve of her dress and handed it to Ailis. "I will distract it here as best I can, to allow you time and freedom to perform this act." She paused, then caught Ailis's gaze with her own. "For the land, if not for me, witch-child." She smiled wryly. "For Arthur, if you must. But do it, and do it swiftly, before my companion forces me to act."

TEN

"Sir, we *must* go!"

Sir Matthias clearly was not of the same opinion. He stood behind his field desk, a complicated wooden affair covered with maps and missives weighted down by rocks, and stared impassively at Ailis, squinting in the early morning sunlight. "I forbid it."

Frustrated, Ailis turned to Gerard. Gerard felt helpless, but gamely stepped forward.

"Sir, I know how it sounds, truly. And from anyone else I would not believe this story myself. But Ailis is right. Morgain would not come to us without dire need—she is too proud, too haughty. Anything which frightens her should frighten us. And if that means helping her . . . in battle, often enemies become allies, and allies enemies, is that not true?"

Sir Matthias grunted, but did not agree or disagree. Emboldened, Gerard went on. "This is a great danger to us all. How can we say no to her request? Especially if it does, in fact, place her in our debt, somehow?"

"Courtier," Newt muttered to the salamander again curled around his neck, but he did so quietly, and with a small amount of respect. Sir Matthias was listening to the squire's words, at least, which was more than he had done for Ailis's impassioned but emotional outburst.

But the next words from Matthias's mouth dashed those hopes. "Lad, I have warned you about the dangers of spending too much time with those who would use magic—especially those not to be trusted. Arthur told me of your previous experiences with that woman, and his fears for what dire influence she might have had on you—"

Ailis's indignant yelp of outrage at that comment was quickly muffled behind Newt's hand. Another outburst, and Sir Matthias would not only not listen to them, he would have them locked up somewhere for their own good!

"Sir!"

"Not one more word, Gerard." The four were

alone in the space outside Sir Matthias's tent, although a few of the squires were hanging just within earshot, clearly hoping to catch some juicy bit of gossip. Knowing that, Matthias lowered his voice. "You have been given great leeway, in light of your service to the king. But you are still a squire. And these other two do not even have that excuse! Now, be silent, and no more talking with Morgain, or I shall be forced to return you to Camelot!"

"You do that!" Ailis said, having finally wiggled free of Newt's hold. "You just do that! Better yet, let me save you the effort of sending us back!

"Merlin!" She called up into the sky, the power and venom in her voice making Sir Matthias step back involuntarily and cross himself, and sending most of the eavesdropping squires fleeing. "Merlin, you talk to me *right now*! I know you can hear me, blast you. Answer!"

The blast of power that came through her voice was echoed in a low, rolling peal of thunder off in the distance. Ailis blinked, a little surprised at herself, but did not back down.

Out of the thunder there came a higher-pitched noise: the scream of a bird of prey, swooping down on an unsuspecting hare. From the sky came a great, shadowy form, plummeting to land on the grass next to Ailis.

A fleeting shimmer, and the bird's wings extended and the torso grew, and grew, the body turning and twisting on itself as the astral bird became the figure of a man.

Merlin had answered.

"By all the old oak, girl, I'm busy!" He glared at Ailis, clearly expecting her to apologize. She glared right back.

"Tell . . . Sir Matthias"—the honorific came with difficulty from her, she was so angry—"that we need to go. Morgain asked us for help, Merlin! How can we refuse?"

Merlin blinked, his craggy face not losing an inch of its irritation, but refocusing with visible effort on the here and now. In her frustration, she had clearly forgotten that he had no idea what she was talking about. "Right. Hold a moment." He reached out with one hand and touched the side of her face with his fingertips, a single feather falling from his skin as he did so. "Think hard what you need to tell me," he commanded her.

The two boys and the knight waited while Merlin took what he needed from her memory. When his hand dropped and Ailis's eyes opened again, Newt realized that he had been holding his breath.

"Absolutely out of the question."

"What? But Morgain said—"

"Morgain says many things. Few of them are to be trusted. Ailis, *think*, girl. Do you really believe that I would endanger Britain this way? If Morgain's life were truly so necessary to the land's well-being, wouldn't I have dealt with that already?"

Merlin was making a great deal of sense, and Newt could feel his own commitment begin to wane. Morgain was not, after all, to be trusted. Merlin had sworn to protect the land as well.

"Merlin!" Ailis was less willing to listen.

"She is *not* to be trusted, Ailis. Her touch is poison, her malice is toward all beings in Camelot without equal. She hates Arthur and all people affiliated with him, and you are not immune to her. No. I forbid it. I forbid it. You are *not* to leave this camp."

Something heavy settled over them, thickening the air. And for an instant, Newt could not breathe. He was being forced down, forced away from himself, somehow. A red haze began to rise over his eyes, making it impossible for him to think, only follow.

Something stirred in his blood, deep and heavy, and he beat it down. Anger had never served him, not once, and he would not let it rise up and master him now.

"I refuse your geas," Ailis said, raising her hands as though to throw off that heaviness, and suddenly Newt could breathe again, the red haze fading as quickly as it had risen, his normal, rational thoughts taking over once again. "You will not take our choices away from us!"

"Ailis!"

"No, Merlin." She met his look again, head-on. "You will not remove our choices from us. Not by force, and not by magic. Not ever."

And with that, she turned and walked away from the group.

"Women!" Merlin muttered, and with an upward swing of his arms, leapt back into feathered form, rising like an arrow back into the sky and disappearing before he reached the first cloud.

Gerard looked at Newt to read his reaction. Sir Matthias was spluttering in confusion as to what had just happened. Without speaking, Newt turned on his heel and walked away, leaving Gerard to try and calm the knight down.

* * *

Hours later, Gerard was finally able to slip away from Sir Matthias, who had seemed determined to fill the squire's every moment with errands and small, foolish details. He found Ailis, as expected, back by the fire where Morgain had first summoned them the night before.

She was sitting cross-legged in front of the now dead fire, her trousers visible underneath her skirt. She had not been wearing them before. Her long red hair was braided around her head, the way Morgain had been wearing hers, and a leather sack was on the ground in front of her.

"What happened back there?" he asked, sitting beside her, feeling exhaustion pull at him. They had not slept much the night before, and as dusk rapidly approached, his limbs became heavier, and his brain more fogged.

"Merlin tried to put a geas on us." Gerard looked at her blankly. "It's a spell that would not allow us to leave the camp."

"You broke it?"

Ailis nodded. "I suppose I did, yes." She saw Gerard's look, and shrugged. "I was very angry. And

I *know* Merlin; I know how his mind works, so I had an advantage—besides, he wasn't expecting me to do it."

"And now?"

"I'm still angry."

"At Merlin." He hoped. He didn't think he had done anything for her to be angry about. He was occasionally stupid, but he'd never tried to manipulate or force anyone into doing something against their will.

"Yes, mostly. At everyone, but especially Merlin, for being such a hypocrite. Ger, I don't believe that Morgain was lying. I think she was truly scared. And anything that scares her . . ."

"Scares me, too," Gerard admitted. It was the truth.

"I'm going," she said without further comment.

"Obviously," Gerard said dryly, and placed his own bag down on the ground next to hers. He sat down beside her. "We can't take the horses." They didn't own the horses they had been riding; they were loans from Arthur's stable. Going without permission for an emergency, they could justify borrowing the beasts. Leaving against explicit orders . . . that would be theft. There was a moral line he was very clear about not crossing.

"I know," Ailis said. "I think I can work something once we're outside of camp. But I won't know until I try it."

She hesitated, then added, "I'm stronger than I was before. Calling Merlin . . . I *pulled* him from the sky, Gerard. Even knowing him, I shouldn't have been able to do that."

"You think it's Morgain?"

"Actually, I think it's Newt's salamander."

Gerard laughed. Then he realized that she *wasn't* laughing. She wasn't even smiling.

"The salamander?"

"It climbed into a fire and wasn't consumed. It was attracted to my magic. Clearly it's magical, somehow."

"But it prefers Newt, not you." The moment he said it, Gerard realized his mistake in pointing that out. But she only sighed.

"Yes, I had noticed that. And yes," she said with reluctance, "I am . . ."

"Jealous?"

"Jealous," she admitted. "A little. Mostly, I just don't understand it. Newt *hates* magic. He doesn't trust it. But . . ."

She rested her head against his shoulder for a moment. Gerard felt an absurd sense of loss. He grew nostalgic for the days of their youth.

"Go talk to him," he said finally. "Maybe . . . maybe he's been feeding it tidbits, or something. Or maybe salamanders notoriously like the stink of horseflesh on humans."

That got a faint laugh out of her. "We *all* stink of horse at the end of the day, Gerard. Except those who smell worse."

"Talk to him."

"And say what? Newt, I know you hate magic, but that pet you're so fond of? It's magic, completely magic. In fact, it might even be made of magic."

"He liked the griffin," Gerard offered, referring to the great beast they encountered at Morgain's keep, a beast that had kept Ailis company while she was held hostage there.

Ailis made a small, mysterious smile, but merely said, "Sir Tawny wasn't a pet. Not *his* pet, anyway." She clarified. "Newt wasn't carrying him around with him." She shrugged, throwing the question off. "I'll worry about it when we get back. Are you ready to go?"

"Ready as I can be, walking into a probable trap

without Merlin's protection or the king's blessing or any backup save ourselves . . ." Gerard got to his feet, picked up his pack, and offered Ailis a hand as she stood up as well. "You're the one with the map. Where are we going? And how are we getting there?"

Suddenly Newt was standing behind them, his pack on his back and the salamander's head sticking out from inside. If he had overheard any of their conversation, his face didn't show it.

"What, you thought I wasn't coming?" he asked, seeing their astonished expressions. "We've always been in this together."

Ailis smiled and handed Newt the map, and walked off, trusting them to follow her. He unrolled it and scanned the markings quickly.

"That's . . ."

"Uh-huh," Ailis said.

Newt handed the map to Gerard, and hurried to catch up with the serving girl.

"Do you know how long it will take us to get there?"

Gerard looked at the map, and muttered a curse. The area marked, their destination, was a familiar one. A cave in the far northern highlands; the cave where they had found one of the pieces of the talisman that had broken Morgain's sleep-spell.

That cave was home to the dragon Gerard had promised to return and fight, on the day he was made a knight.

"How are we going to get there?" Gerard asked, his voice rising in dismay. At least it didn't crack like the first time they had encountered the dragon, and his voice had still been changing.

"Maybe we won't even see the dragon. Maybe whatever we're looking for is outside the cave." And maybe this was all a cruel joke on Morgain's part, sending them there. He wouldn't put that past her at all.

"It's going to take us forever to get there," Newt said, echoing his thoughts.

"Don't you two trust me?" Ailis asked, waving in passing to one of the knights standing on the perimeter of the camp, as though the three of them were simply out for an evening's walk. Hopefully the fact that they were not leading horses would cause the guards to overlook their saddlebags.

"I hate it when someone asks me that," Newt said to Gerard. "Don't you?"

"We're not walking," Gerard guessed. "Ailis . . ."

His half-formed suspicion about the cause of Ailis's earlier smile was correct. There, crouched in the shadows cast by the afternoon sun, his stunning golden feathers glinting in the light, was Sir Tawny, the griffin Ailis had befriended during her stay in Morgain's keep.

"Morgain's sending us to do her business," Ailis said. "She won't mind if we borrow him for a little while."

"We're going to . . . ride that?" Newt looked like he wasn't sure if he should be nervous or excited.

"Unless you want him to carry you in his claws all the way."

"I don't think so, no," he said, shaking his head. "Riding will be . . . fine."

Ailis laughed at him, going forward to greet the griffin. The great beast's head, shaped like an eagle's but as large as a draft horse's, ducked to meet her, allowing her access to the feathers tufted over its ears, keeping the fiercer curved beak from her soft flesh.

"We're going to ride *that* . . ." Newt's tone had gone from disbelief to awe. There was a makeshift rope harness attached to the creature's catlike body, with knotted loops where feet and hands could be inserted for gripping, but otherwise there was no saddle, no reins, no way to stay on or control the winged beast.

"I think I'm going to be sick," Gerard said.

*　*　*

As it turned out, Gerard was fine, straddling Sir Tawny's neck, staring down at the villages they flew over, trying to estimate the size of each one by how many rooftops he could count, while Ailis clung to the other side of the griffin and whispered in his ear, encouraging him to fly just a little longer, just a little farther, there was a good boy.

Newt, clinging to the rope harness, wondered if closing his eyes was better than keeping them open, and tried not to throw up on the poor, patient griffin's feathers.

"Look at that!" Gerard called out. "Over there!"

"No," Newt moaned, refusing to look.

"It's all right," Ailis said, the wind carrying her words back to him. "We're here. Hold on . . ."

"What do you think I've been doing?" Newt asked, then gulped and turned a deeper shade of green as the griffin banked and folded his wings, going into a steep descent, right into the side of a mountain. Even knowing that there was a plateau there, where they had left their horses during the first visit, didn't make Newt believe they were going to land as anything other than a splat against the rocks.

"You can open your eyes now," Ailis said in his ear, while trying to stifle her laughter. They were safe and on solid ground.

"I hate both of you," Newt said as he opened his eyes, pried his fingers off the rope harness, and swung his still-shaky legs over the griffin's side.

"Thank you, Sir Tawny," Ailis said, giving the creature's feathers a final stroke. "If you can stay, that would be wonderful, but we understand if you cannot."

"We do?" Gerard said, then took a step back when Sir Tawny swung that great head to look him directly in the eye. "Of course. Thank you, Sir Tawny. Your aid is most appreciated." He made a shallow bow to the griffin, and turned away to examine the cave's entrance.

The salamander, which had hidden at the bottom of Newt's sack the entire trip, chose that moment to stick its green head out and extend its tongue at the griffin. The creature made a noise of indifference, and launched itself into the air, wings beating so heavily the gust almost knocked Ailis over.

"Right," Newt said, looking around, and relishing the feel of solid stone under his feet. "Let's get this done."

ELEVEN

"That may be more difficult than we thought," Gerard said, pointing. The arched entrance into the hill they had used the last time was now blocked by rubble. There were huge, heavy boulders and smaller rocks, the spaces between filled with smaller pebbles and stones.

"Rockslide," he continued, looking up the mountain. "Recent, but not the past few days. All the dust has settled, and the grit's wedged in . . . it's rained since then."

"So how are *we* supposed to get in?" Newt asked. He tried to move one of the moderate-sized rocks with his hands, and failed. "You'd need draft horses—a team of them—to get this cleared."

"Or magic," Ailis said, shouldering her way past them. Staring at the pile of rocks, she clenched and opened her hands a few times, thinking, then held her palms up facing the pile, fingers curled in slightly, and whispered something in a language neither boy understood.

A few pebbles shifted and fell, but otherwise there was no reaction.

Ailis repeated the spell, speaking louder, with more specific enunciation.

A rock shifted uneasily, but did not move from its wedged-in nook.

"That isn't going to work," Newt said finally, watching sweat break out on Ailis's forehead. She wasn't quite as strong as she thought she was. He wondered for a moment if there was something keeping those rocks in place.

"Is there any other way in?" was all he asked, out loud.

"Not according to this map, no," Gerard said.

"I don't remember any other way the last time, either," Newt admitted.

"So either we get in through here, or we go home, having failed." Ailis set her jaw in a stubborn line. "That's *not* an option."

She walked up to the rockslide, and traced an oval on the rocks with her fingertips, measuring in her mind. Then she stepped back, took a deep breath, and made a motion with her hands, as though she were pushing something, hard, with both hands.

The salamander poked its head out from under Newt's collar and looked over his shoulder, seemingly fascinated with what Ailis was doing.

"Help me," she whispered to it, and the creature crawled forward a bit more, its narrow tongue flicking out as though tasting the air—or the energy coming off Ailis.

"As I see it happening, let it happen. As I will it, so mote it be."

There was a shimmer in the air, and then a ring of fire appeared, etching into the stones where Ailis had traced the oval. The flames burned white, then blue, then a deep, watery sea green, filling in the oval until the stones were a sheet of fire. All three humans had to turn away, or risk damaging their eyesight. When they looked back, a door had been forced in the rock, just large enough for them to step through.

"Nice," Gerard said, and stepped forward without hesitation, his right hand resting casually on the hilt of his sword. Ailis was directly behind him. Newt followed a step more slowly, pausing to run a hand along the edge of the hole. The rocks were fused along the rim into a smooth whole, as though it had always been one piece.

"Very nice," he said, impressed despite himself, as he dropped into the cool darkness of the cave itself.

Inside, he found Ailis on her knees, Gerard trying to lift her up.

"What happened?"

"She just keeled over," Gerard said, clearly concerned. Ailis was sweating even more fiercely now, her skin pale and shining in the darkness.

"Was . . . too much, somehow. I don't know why. I could feel the power . . . and then it just went away, all fast and sudden and . . ."

"And she fell over."

The salamander practically jumped off Newt's neck in his hurry, wiggle-walking to get to Ailis. She automatically put out a hand to catch it.

"Hey . . ."

"No, it's okay," she said. "I think . . . I got some of that from you, didn't I? I was right about you being magic. But away from fire, you can't do much, can you?"

"What?" Newt was confused.

"Ailis thinks . . . from the way it reacted—or didn't react—to fire, it's magical," Gerard explained.

Newt started to protest, then the events came back to him, and his shoulders slumped. "Yeah. Fine. If he helps you, *you* keep him, then."

The salamander made a squeaking noise, and Ailis shook her head. "He's yours. He chose you. I don't think he'd be interested in me at all, except when I'm using magic."

"If you're sure . . ."

She managed to laugh. "*He* is," she said. Sure enough, once Constans had determined that Ailis wasn't doing anything interesting, he seemed determined to crawl back onto Newt's shoulder.

"All right." He reached out to scratch the creature under its wedge-shaped head. "But if you need him . . ."

"Friends, we're supposed to be looking for something that will lead us to the shadow figure's true name," Gerard reminded them, with his hand still under Ailis's elbow.

She allowed him to help her up, leaning heavily on his shoulder with a mixture of gratitude and annoyance. She didn't try to stand on her own just yet, but they moved forward together, with Newt and Constans a single step behind.

"Yeah. I'll be okay. Just . . . a little dizzy," she said

as they walked down the wide cavern. The walls were as high and as pale as she remembered, though the footing did not seem quite as smooth.

"Too much magic," Newt said. "You're not as strong as you thought you were."

"You always this sympathetic?" Ailis shot back in return, clearly irritated.

"Yes," Newt replied, pleased to hear the color returning to her voice. "You hadn't noticed?"

"Funny." But she relaxed a little. He could see it in the way she moved.

"Humans!"

The bellow came out of the darkness ahead of them, where the cavern branched off into two smaller tunnels, and Ailis tensed up again immediately. To be fair, all four of them did, Constans included.

"Uh-oh," Ailis said. "Guess he's still around."

"Dragon," Newt explained to the salamander, who dove down the back of his tunic at the sudden, booming noise. "Not like you, even if he does breathe fire. Big fellow, larger than the griffin. Nasty temper, too. And smart. Best stay low in case he eats smaller cousins as well as humans and goats and horses."

"He sounds angry," Ailis noted.

"Well, he wasn't exactly *friendly* the last time,"

Gerard reminded them. "He wanted to eat us, remember?"

"He sounds angrier," Ailis said nervously.

"Humans!"

Gerard had to admit the truth of that. The dragon also sounded like he was getting closer. Fast.

A flare of light deep in the left-hand passage and a blast of warm, foul-smelling air reached them.

"His breath hasn't improved," Newt said, gagging a little.

"Does it smell like he's been . . . eating people recently?" Ailis wondered.

Nobody asked her how they were supposed to know what a man-eater's breath would smell like.

"We could just go the other way," Newt said.

"You mean avoid him?" Gerard asked.

"I mean run."

"We can't." Ailis looked terrified, but was stubborn. Both boys recognized the stubborn part. "If what we're looking for is here, the dragon might know about it."

"And you think he'll tell us? We barely found something to trade with him the last time, remember?" The thing they traded was, in effect, Gerard—or at least a future version of himself. "And we don't even have horses to offer this time, either."

Not that the dragon had been interested in horse-meat then.

The three friends looked at each other, then down the corridor, where the flickering red light was coming closer.

"I think—"

"We should—"

"Probably not bother him," Ailis agreed. They turned to go down the right-hand tunnel when there was a heavy, unnerving noise. Gerard hesitated, and a huge, scaled foot with claws the size of daggers, only twice as thick—and sharp—came out of the darkness at them. It moved with astonishing quickness for something so large, flattening Gerard against the floor. Thankfully, the claws did not puncture anything more than the fabric of his tunic.

"Humans! Come!"

"Maybe . . . we should . . . stop by and pay our . . . respects," Gerard suggested breathlessly, his face turned to avoid breathing in the dust from the stone floor. He sounded like one or more of his ribs might be broken.

"Or we could just leave you to explain," Newt suggested. "Seeing as how you're the one he got along with so well last time.

"All right, it was just an idea," he said hastily, when Ailis and Gerard both glared at him.

The huge dragon's paw started to pull back into the corridor, slowly but inevitably dragging Gerard back with it. Helpless to do anything else, Ailis and Newt followed.

As they walked, the corridor opened into a larger cavern—not the treasure-trove nesting room they had found the dragon in the first time, but it was still impressive for being deep inside a mountain. A red glow came from the tiny flamelets rising from the dragon's nostrils, like torches in the night. Light came down through stone chimneys that must lead all the way up to the surface, carrying faint sunlight down into the depths.

The dragon had drawn Gerard to him the way a cat might a mouse, letting him go once all three were inside the cavern.

It was still magnificent, with its silvery blue scales, and the elongated, muscled body leading to a thick, arched neck and tapered, triangular head. Its eyes glared down at them with something beyond ire, and approaching madness.

"Sir Dragon, we—" Gerard began, rolling out of

immediate reach and getting up onto his knees, crouching in a pose of nonaggressive readiness. "We did not—"

"Silence!"

Gerard shut up.

"You have returned." The dragon's voice softened to a cold rumble. It sniffed the air, steam and more firelets rising from his great nostrils as he did so. "You are a knight, now?"

"Not yet, no. I—"

"You lie! I was told that you would lie!" A dragon's roar was bad enough when heard at a distance. In close quarters, in an echoing stone cavern, it was so terrible as to make the bones in your head vibrate.

"I do not lie!" Gerard protested, stung by the accusation.

Ailis, more practically, asked, "Who told you that he would lie?"

"You have reneged. You never planned to honor your bargain."

"Sir Dragon, I had—have—no intention of reneging. If I had, why would I return now? Unready, yes, I am, but also honest. I am a human of my word. My *good* word."

The dragon did not seem appeased. Nor did it

answer Ailis's question.

"You have returned. We will have our battle. *Now*."

That had been the bargain they had made the last time: They wanted the piece of the talisman they needed, which the dragon possessed. The dragon had wanted fame and glory, of the sort which could come only from a great battle with a knight of reputation.

Gerard had promised to return when he was made a knight and give the dragon that battle to the death.

They had not anticipated that the dragon would not believe—or care—that Gerard was not yet a knight.

"Face me, human. Or die like a sheep, bleating in fear."

The dragon, with its own sort of honor, was ignoring Newt and Ailis. She was frantically searching her memory for any kind of spell or magic that could get them out of this, but it was one thing to melt rocks, call a beast, or even force Merlin to come speak to her. It was another to try and affect such a huge, intelligent, powerful, *angry* creature—especially when it was well within claw-swipe distance. Even a halfhearted blow from that paw, and she would never work any magic ever again.

How in heaven's name could Gerard muster anything against it? Yes, he had taken Morgain down, sword to sword, but she had chosen not to work magic, and to face him on his own terms. The dragon would have no such limitations.

"Go stand against the far wall," Gerard told them, getting to his feet.

"Ger, we can—"

"No." Gerard stopped whatever Newt was going to offer. "This is mine to do. You two—whatever happens, you still have to find what we're here for. You can't afford to fail."

He got to his feet, slowly and deliberately brushing himself off. He made sure that his sword belt was still secured, and that his weapons had taken no damage during his undignified entrance to the cavern.

Watching him, Ailis realized that he was imagining that he was Sir Lancelot. Not now, when he was known to be such a great and gallant fighter, the king's best-loved knight, but back before, when he first came to Camelot and was mocked for being honest, for being awkward and homely. A great knight Lancelot might be, but he would never be handsome. But Sir Lancelot knew that, and cared not, so long as in battle he could be glorious. Gerard was handsome, or would be, but like Lancelot he cared more for his actions than his appearance.

Ailis was terrified for her oldest friend. But she was proud of him, too. So when he looked her way, briefly, she gave him a brave smile and a nod. *You'll do what needs to be done,* she thought. *And so will we. Don't worry about us.*

Then she took Newt's hand, tugging at him until he moved away with her, giving the two, knight and dragon, room to face each other.

"If Gerard . . ."

"He won't. And if he does . . . we take his sword back to Arthur, and tell him his man fought bravely, and well." Her words stuck in her throat. "But first we have to find what we came for."

They came upon a niche in the wall that was large enough for both of them to fit in, and made themselves as comfortable as possible. They might have gone on, leaving Gerard to his fate and made use of the time. But while they were willing to go on afterward, they would not leave him now.

"Sir Dragon," Gerard said, standing in the open space before the dragon, looking up to the proud head, the long, sinuous neck, the great, scaled body. "I have returned, as promised, to give you what challenge this human form might offer—and to win."

Dragon laughter came out in smoke rings.

"Come then, human. Give me a challenge."

Back when he worked in the kennels, Newt used to wade into the middle of dogfights, breaking up even the most vicious-situation with a clout to the head or a swing of a stick. He didn't think that there was anything that could unnerve him. But watching Gerard draw his sword—an ordinary, dark-edged length of metal, nothing flashy or enchanted—against the muscled, dangerous bulk of the dragon made him shiver.

"I can't watch," he said, but yet was unable to turn his head away.

The dragon lunged, his long neck darting like a serpent, the great head coming in far too close to Gerard's body. But the boy knew it for a feint, ignoring the snapping teeth in favor of the foreleg which also came in, claws outstretched. His sword hit against one claw, slid along the length of it, and sliced into the scaled pad underneath, causing thick purple blood to well up from the cut.

First blooding went to Gerard. The dragon didn't seem at all bothered by it.

Then the battle began in earnest, and Newt could barely follow the action. Ailis's occasional comments made him realize that she knew far more of battle techniques than he did. He could tell you how to train a horse to perform moves with a knight on horseback, and how to treat the wounds incurred in battle, but he had never bothered to watch the moves being performed. Ailis, with her time spent in Camelot proper, had seen more tournaments.

She had, in fact, lived through a real battle, the one in which she was orphaned. That thought made Newt's arm around her shoulder tighten, to offer comfort, but she didn't seem to even notice.

"Oh, good move, that was—no! Oh." A sigh of relief, as Gerard spun and escaped the claw, parrying with the flat of his blade. The noises filling the cavern were a mixture of heavy slapping thuds of feet, the clang of metal against claw, and the sound of Gerard's breathing, which was becoming more and more labored. A bad blow with one paw had left his right arm at a painful-looking angle. He switched the sword to his left arm, and continued fighting.

"He can't . . ." Newt started to say.

"He *will*," Ailis said fiercely, but without confidence.

He couldn't, of course. Perhaps not even the best of knights could have, not against a full-grown dragon. After all, were they not so deadly, they would not be so feared.

"No!" Newt wasn't sure who had cried out, Ailis or himself, or both. Gerard went down, a gash across his left leg bleeding through his clothing.

The dragon raised itself to full height, clearly savoring the moment.

Gerard got up on his uninjured leg, using the sword as a crutch, and stared back at the dragon. His body shook, but his gaze was steady. Newt tried to look anywhere else rather than see what was about to happen. He noticed that the sunlight coming down into the chamber had strengthened—the sun must have been at such an angle as to shine directly into the opening. One beam in particular caught Gerard's form, casting a long narrow darkness against the blood-splattered ground.

"The Grail hides in shadows, in long dark shadows. Bring the light, and dispel the shadows. Find the Grail."

He couldn't remember why the words echoed in his head at that exact moment. Brother Jannot. Long dark shadows. The Grail. Bring the light, and dispel the shadows.

The dragon had already led the way to one talisman—perhaps it knew the whereabouts of a second, too. Newt wondered how to dispel the darkness. *Have Ailis set another fire? But how, without further angering the dragon? What to do?* His thoughts were chasing each other in frantic movements—anything to keep from thinking about Gerard and what was about to happen.

"Not a great battle, not one to speak of through the ages, but satisfying nonetheless," the dragon said in its deep, rumbling voice. "Will you beg for mercy, now?"

"Abide . . . abide by honor," was all Gerard said. "Allow my companions to go on their way, with no hindrance, and finish this."

"That is your only word?" The dragon sounded almost disappointed. "You will not beg?"

"For my companions, on your honor," Gerard repeated, placing his blood-caked sword on the ground before him. "For myself, nothing save a worthy ending."

The dragon studied him, then nodded with what looked almost to be a sneer. "Prettily said. I don't believe a word of it, but despite what the shadowed one said, you did come back and honor your vow, and the way you die does matter to you humans, so I will grant that last request."

All of Gerard's dreams, his visions of glory, of being the one to find the Grail, save the fair maiden, capture the evildoer, win renown as the bravest, wisest, most wonderful of Arthur's knights . . . it all faded, and he let it go.

What mattered was the here and now. All that mattered was that he fulfill his promise, no matter how mistaken the dragon might be about his worth.

All that mattered now was that Ailis and Newt be free to continue with their own quest, and that Morgain be freed from her unholy bargain, that the threat to the kingdom be removed. He heard Ailis's cry, Newt's voice in response, but it was all distant as Camelot, now.

Gerard made his peace with all of that, and bent his head to receive the fatal blow.

*   *   *

Newt thought that he was imagining it, at first: that the strain had made him hallucinate. Then Ailis's cry showed that she had heard it as well. A chiming noise, gentle as a summer's breeze, clear as a moonlit night. It made him feel as though all the joy had left the world, and then returned but through a different door.

It filled the cavern, every span of it, echoing off the walls, sinking into the air they breathed, their skin, bones, and blood. It made Newt remember, for the first time in years, his mother's tears.

He looked up, eyes wide, and saw the dragon rearing back even farther, its head rising to the roof of the cavern, its expression astonished and angry.

The chime sounded again, rising as the echoes of the first peal faded, and the dragon's entire body convulsed, the twitch beginning in its gut, working all the way up its massive torso. Newt could almost see each scale bulge and ripple as something terrible happened within the dragon's body, rising all the way up the dragon's long, sinewy neck.

"He looks"—not even the glory of the sound could stop the comment from coming out of his mouth—"like he's going to throw up!"

The dragon shook its head, swinging its neck back and forth, as though trying to deny whatever was happening. A third chime sounded, this time more insistent, and Ailis gasped. "It's coming from *inside* the dragon!"

Even as they both realized the origin of the

sound, the dragon's mouth opened, and a blast of flame emerged.

Cold flame. Newt realized even as he shielded Ailis with his body. Constans rose up on his shoulder, its neck stretched out to greet the fire, a smaller, more slender version of the dragon. His tongue flicked out in anticipation.

The flame broke over the salamander like water flowing around a sword, and flowed past them as formless and gentle as a mother's kiss.

Newt dared to look over his shoulder, and his jaw fell open. Whatever shocks, whatever surprises he had dealt with until now were nothing compared to the sight of what was being belched from the dragon's gut.

It landed a few paces from them, the glow dissipating from around it as it fell. The dragon's body folded in on itself, the great neck coiling back down onto its shoulders, torso and tail curling into a sleeping pose. The glaring eyes flickered shut.

Newt held his breath. The dragon did not move.

The last remnant of the chimes faded entirely, leaving behind nothing but a patient silence.

"Ailis." Newt's voice was hoarse, as though he had been screaming for months. He cleared his

throat, wincing at how much it hurt, and tried again. "Ailis."

She opened her eyes, pulling away from Newt's protective hug, and looked around, visibly bracing herself for the sight of Gerard, sprawled lifeless and bloody on the cavern floor.

He was bloody, yes, but still breathing. At least until he looked up and saw the dragon, no longer any threat to him. His skin flushed, then went white, and he fell back to his knees, wincing in pain as he did so.

"We did it," he said in awe. "We found the Grail."

"From the body of the last dragon left in England," Newt said, getting to his feet and walking over on wobbly legs, looking down in wonder.

It was such a simple thing: a plain wooden goblet, scratched and battered from use and age. The wood was dark, with a purple-tinged grain.

"Olivewood," Newt said, then blinked, surprised that he had known it.

Gerard reached out to touch it, then stopped. It was just a cup, a thing that would have looked totally ordinary next to any knight's trencher back in Camelot. But there was no doubt among them what it truly was.

"I wonder if the dragon swallowed it, thinking it was treasure . . . or if someone put it there, for safe-keeping." Ailis had gone directly to Gerard, check-ing his leg, then his arm. She tried to pull strips off her skirt in order to create a bandage. The fabric was tough to tear, so she pulled Gerard's dagger from his belt without him even noticing, using it to slice at the fabric.

"For safekeeping? Ow!" He complained as she tied the makeshift bandage around his leg.

"It makes as much sense as hiding it in a forest," she retorted, taking refuge in arguing. "Maybe . . . maybe the dragon's being magical itself, by its very nature, hid the magic of the Grail . . ."

"How?" Gerard asked.

"Things magical. They feel different." She didn't know how else to explain what she could see so clearly. "I can feel it now, coming off the Grail. I couldn't sense it before, like the dragon blocked it. But what made the dragon give it up? And why is it sleeping now?"

"Who cares?" Gerard's pain and defeat was for-gotten as he stared at the prize. "We did it. We won the Grail!"

Ailis pulled the second bandage around his arm tighter than she might have. "Don't say that."

"Why not?"

"I told you, back when Arthur first announced this entire Quest idea. The Grail's not something to be won. It has to be earned. How many times do I have to tell you *anything* before you listen?"

Gerard dimly remembered her saying something like that. He and Mak had been discussing their slim chances of being taken along on the Quest, and she had come along and doused their schemes and plans.

"We were here when the dragon coughed it up," Newt said. "That has to count for something."

"I think . . ." Ailis looked at Gerard, speculatively. "I think Ger's willingness to do the right thing, facing the dragon like he promised, had something to do with it."

He could feel his face turning red. Now that the danger was passed, his thoughts and emotions felt overdone, silly.

"But all it did was make the dragon pass along the Grail," she went on. "It didn't *give* it to us."

"There's a difference?" Newt seemed uncertain.

"There is." On that point, she was definite. "None of us is a bad person—we're all pretty good, actually. Loyal. Brave. But we're not without sin. We're not . . . Sir Galahad, for example." Sir Galahad the Pure, as he was known throughout the land, was said to never argue, never fuss, but was serene and mild even under the worst conditions. It was very irritating to most of his fellow knights, even as they admired his piety and goodness.

"If what you're saying is true, though, I did earn it," Gerard insisted. But his voice was uncertain, and his gaze flickered around the cavern, settling on anything except the Grail, as though it might rise up and refute him.

"You freed it. Or called it. But if we earned it, why isn't it all glowing or anything, the way it is in all the parchments and tapestries?"

"Maybe because it needs to be held?"

"Then why isn't one of us holding it?"

None of them made a move to be the first to pick it up.

"Isn't not feeling worthy a sign that you're worthy?" Newt suggested.

Both Gerard and Ailis looked at him. "Doesn't matter, anyway. Even if it were glowing and singing hymns and calling down angels, none of it would help unless there happens to be a slip of parchment in there that has what we're looking for. Or did you forget why we're really here?"

"How can you say that?" Gerard was outraged, his former uncertainty giving way to anger that made his spine straighten even against the pain. "The Grail is *everything*. It's what this has all been about!"

Newt bent down and picked the Grail up, his hand closing around the carved stem without hesitation. "To you, to the rest of the knights, sure. It's a relic, maybe even a powerful one. But it's not going to save us from Morgain's companion and whatever it has planned. Only *we* can do that."

They were brave words, and true. Unfortunately, he had no idea what to do. And from the look on his friends' faces, neither did they.

TWELVE

"So . . . What do we do now?" Newt asked.

Ailis looked around, checking carefully around the bulk of the dragon without getting too close. There was nothing that, as far as she was able to determine, could lead them to the name of the shadow-figure. Giving up, she turned to watch her friends.

Newt was helping Gerard hobble a few steps. Then he stopped and tested the bandages she had tied. The bleeding had stopped, for the most part, and his sword was doing decent second duty as a crutch, which was almost more painful to Gerard, she suspected, than the wounds themselves. They'd have to go slowly, but he would be able to travel.

"Morgain said the answer was here—a Well of Bitter Water." Again, the reference tickled at her memory, but nothing came of it. "Whatever that is, it's not in this room . . . so we must go on."

"And the Grail?" Gerard asked.

"It waited for decades, inside a dragon's gut," she said, reluctant but practical. "It can wait a little while longer."

"And if we don't make it?" Gerard didn't intend for it to sound so harsh, but the question had to be asked.

"We make sure that we make it," Newt said firmly. "Agreed?"

"I can agree to that," Ailis said, and Gerard nodded his own reluctant agreement. He longed to take the Grail to Arthur, but what would be the point, if abandoning Morgain's charge left them at the mercy of the companion's evil plans?

"So," Newt said. "There are no ways out except the way we came in. So we go back and take the other passage."

He looked around for a place to put the Grail, but his pack was already overfull, thanks to Constans taking up residence there again. The urge to give it to Ailis, rather than let Gerard hold it, flashed through his brain, and he squelched it. The squire would not abandon them to return to Camelot with his prize. Of all three of them, Gerard had risked the most, going against Sir Matthias, facing down the dragon. He had earned the right to carry it, if nothing else. Besides, it would give him something to think about other than the pain, which had to be intense.

"Let's go."

As they walked, Newt felt a strange sense of unease crawling in his veins. Constans seemed to be twitchy as well, crawling out of the pack slung against the boy's back and up to the top of Newt's head in order to see better. After the salamander deliberately dug his claws into Newt's scalp a few times when Newt took specific turns, the boy shrugged and started letting the lizard lead them. It was no worse a way of choosing direction than any other, he supposed.

Constans led them down branch after branch of the main artery, each hallway becoming narrower and darker.

"Your head is glowing," Ailis noted once. Newt's shaggy black hair was indeed lit from underneath—specifically where Constans was. The salamander's skin was emitting a faint glow, which picked up the highlights and made it seem as though Newt's hair were made of low-burning twigs, or faint flames.

"There are women back in Camelot who would pay good money to make their hair do that," Ailis said. "Perhaps when we get back, you could sell Constans to them."

"Sell?" Newt clutched at his heart dramatically, as though horrified she could suggest such a thing.

"All right then, loan. For favors in return."

Favors were the coin of the court, in many ways; that and gossip. Newt seriously doubted that any of the ladies would be willing to owe him anything even for the use of the salamander. But it was an amusing thought to pass time while they walked through dark, stone hallways, trying not to wonder too much about what they would find—if anything.

"Wait." Gerard stopped, resting with the sword's point digging a scratch into the soft rock of the floor under his weight. "Do you smell that?"

"What?"

"Saltwater," Newt said, sniffing the air as well.

"In the middle of a mountain?" Ailis blinked, looking between the two of them. "Bitter water . . ."

That had been the phrase she was trying to remember. Back in the Queen's solar, what seemed like a lifetime ago, a young singer had recited a poem from an earlier generation, about a sailor's sweet-heart longing for the scent of sea to remind her of the man she missed.

"And bitter water she cried into the well
Calling the shape of her master
Mastering the water the waves he rode
And wishing him home on the next tide."

They picked up the pace as best they could with Gerard's leg slowing them down. Another turn, and the smell of the water mixed with something sweeter but equally sharp.

"Oh."

"That's . . . unexpected," Newt said dryly, holding his nose, while Constans hissed in what might have been agreement or pleasure.

The passageway broadened suddenly into a bright cavern so large they could not see the ceiling or the sides. A grove of trees grew in the center, their roots digging directly into the rock as though it were the richest soil.

Newt started listing off the trees he saw there: "Rowan, oak, yew—lots of yew. Ash, hazel—none of these should be growing here. None of them should be growing together."

"Hush," Ailis said, but it was impossible to be

annoyed, not in the face of the miracle in front of them.

"This . . . this is where I would have expected to find the Grail," Gerard said slowly.

"I wonder if the dragon came from here, too," Newt said. "I never quite understood why it would want to live within stone. If there's drinking water here, as well as bitter . . ."

Ailis walked forward, drawn toward the well in the center of the grove. Constans slipped off Newt's shoulder, twisting as he fell, then disappeared into the thick grass that grew around the well.

The flat stones that made up the well were pitted and pockmarked with age, and curved in a way that was not found in nature, but yet showed no obvious marks of chisel or hatchet.

"Like the stone in your doorway," Gerard said.

Ailis nodded, running her fingers over the stones as though trying to read them through her skin. "This isn't magic, though. Or if it is, it's very very old. So old that all traces of its magic have worn off. Or it may be some kind of magic I don't know . . . It's lovely. So very lovely."

"And *not* drinking water." Newt had reached down and cupped a handful of the impossibly turquoise water and sipped it, then spat it out on the grass. "Salt. This is ocean water. Only . . . it's warm."

"Sun-warmed?" Ailis suggested, clearly still entranced by the feel of the stones.

"What sun?" he asked in return.

That was a good point. There was light in here, diffused and hazy, but definitely not sunlight. The trees grew, the grass grew, the water was warmed . . . and they were inside a mountain.

"I hate magic," Newt said. "It . . . complicates everything."

"What's the difference between magic and a miracle?" Gerard wondered, touching the Grail, safe in his pack, with the hand not gripping his sword-crutch. They had had this discussion once before. He had thought that faith was something you just had, like brown eyes, or the ability to run fast. A lot had happened since then. A lot had been seen and experienced since then. He wasn't as sure of his answers as he used to be.

"A miracle has no explanation," Ailis said softly. "Magic has a cause, a reason." She had seen a lot, too. Somehow, along the way, she had become more certain, while he became less so.

"So what are we looking for, exactly?" Newt leaned over the well's mouth, trying to see if anything was written on the stones inside. "A name? A picture? Oh, there's something written here."

And Newt was still Newt: solid, dependable, practical; a good person to have on your side.

He pulled back out of the well, looking at his black-smudged fingers. "It's soot. There are all these markings down there. I can't see what they are exactly, but they seem to be written in soot. Looks like they haven't been there very long. Or maybe the water's keeping them from disappearing. I don't know."

"A spell. Morgain's spell," Ailis said. "The one she said she used to call the companion." It was a guess, but a reasonable one. "Come here!"

The two boys turned to see what she was pointing at. A small fire pit, just beyond the grass. The coals had been carefully banked, but they were still glowing.

"Someone left a fire burning?" Newt sounded outraged.

"The stones are cold," she noted, bending down. "So are the ashes." Her hand held over the coals. "The coals are hot, though. It's *just* been banked."

Something—the smell of the wind, a rustle, a change of air pressure—made Ailis stand up and turn around quickly.

"Morgain!"

But this was not the Morgain of worried confidences. This was not even the thoughtful teacher of magic.

Clad in a gown of deepest violet, a band of gold and silver held her heavy black locks in place, and thicker bands of silver were seen at her neck and wrists. This was Morgain the Queen. Morgain the Enchantress.

Morgain Le Fay.

Ailis saw her and was afraid.

"Morgain?" she said again, reaching with voice and magic to the woman behind the coldly perfect face, the coolly impassive eyes.

And then a figure appeared behind the enchantress: cowled and dark, menacing, here in this place of unexpected beauty.

Ailis took a step backward, almost landing in the fire, causing the salamander, who had slithered from the grasses to take refuge in the coals, to hiss in agitation.

"Morgain, behind you . . ."

"You've done well, witch-child." The enchantress's voice was tinged with regret, but only faintly.

"I don't understand. . . ."

"She lied, Ailis." Newt's voice was as cold as

214

Morgain's expression. "Everything was a lie."

"Not everything," the woman replied, smiling in a way that sent shivers down their spines. "I did indeed call my companion forth from this Well of Bitter Waters, with the spell inscribed just inside the rim," and she gestured at their soot-smeared fingers. "And there was certainly a bargain struck, between us two."

She paused. "In fact, had you discovered my companion's name, it would indeed have been a thing of great power over it, enough for me to drive it from these lands. A pity that you did not have time to succeed."

The shadow-figure behind her glowered at that, but Morgain did not seem to notice. Or perhaps she did not care.

"So no, I did not lie. I simply was not . . . forth-coming about the price that would be required, to pay for the bargain I made."

"Not *your* magic," Gerard said, things suddenly falling into place. He shifted the sword in his hand, testing to see if his leg would support his weight. "Not your blood. *Hers*."

"Indeed." The enchantress nodded her regal head once in acknowledgment.

"Morgain!" Ailis was having trouble accepting what she was hearing.

"It would not have been my first wish, or even my second," Morgain said, meeting Ailis's gaze squarely, without flinching. "But I am reminded that there are sacrifices which need to be made to achieve a final goal."

The companion brought forth a soft envelope of cloth, unrolled it, and placed it on the ground. It was a map. But it shimmered, and the markings rose from flat ink into shapes and figures above the parchment that seemed to be moving.

Newt took a cautious step back, even as Ailis leaned forward, fascinated.

Morgain's cold voice warmed, slightly. "You will become part of a new world, Ailis. Not gone, but reformed. A world in which the Old Ways are honored once again, where men are not the sole leaders, the sole rulers. A world in which women reclaim their rightful place, their rightful powers."

"But I won't be around to see it," Ailis said, shaking her head. The shadow-figure, who had moved closer to her, hissed.

"That can be done without death," Newt said. Despite his own fear, he inched forward to take her arm, move her farther away from the triple threat of Morgain, her companion, and the map. The companion turned its glare on him, and did not back down. "Ailis, I know it's appealing, but think—"

Ailis found an outlet for her conflicting emotions. Turning on Newt, she said, "Appealing? What do you think of me?" She turned to Morgain, then. "And you. You speak of women having power. Where is *my* power, Morgain? Where is *my* right to decide what I want to do?"

"Child . . ."

"No!" Ailis knew that it was useless, but just as it had when facing Merlin, the anger she felt now reformed as power and welled up inside her. She felt it burn in her veins, a twitch forcing her arm out, throwing that power at Morgain.

The enchantress caught the spear magic easily, absorbing it without more expression than a gently raised eyebrow.

"I'm sorry, Ailis. But the end result will be worth it."

"What about the Grail?" Ailis shouted.

Morgain checked herself mid-gesture. "What of it?" There was a new tone in her voice, a hunger that made Newt shiver, increasing his desire to pull Ailis out of range, out of sight, out of danger.

Ailis only saw that she had the upper hand, at least for the moment. "You said that it was yours more than Arthur's. That its 'blood-infused power' was more Old Ways than New—that it would be enough to bring you to power. Wasn't that part of your plan as well? To find it, use it, to help you find an heir, and save the land?"

Gerard, sensing imminent danger, tried to silence Ailis, but he could not.

"The Grail came to us!" the girl continued, caught up in her anger. "We were deemed worthy enough to carry it, not you."

"Grail? You have the Grail?" Morgain's voice was scornful, but there was a terrible hope in her eyes.

"It matters not." The companion's voice was as terrifying as Ailis remembered: It wasn't heard with the ears as much as it was felt in the spine, crawling like cold fingers and sneaking into the back of her head, sending chills everywhere. "Morgain, I have given you what you desired, what you needed. Even the Grail in their possession cannot save Arthur's kingdom from your wrath. And it cannot unbind our bargain, if you were thinking of that."

"But if I had it . . . we would not need to use the girl. The Grail holds the blood of the land—that has always been its power. It can hold the power, and be the sacrifice instead of her."

Ailis's eyes met Gerard's. He had heard it, too: the tone in Morgain's voice. Not strong, not loud, but a definite note of reluctance. Of wistfulness. Of regret.

The shadow-figure had heard it, too. "Foolish mortal! You wish for everything, without giving up anything. It does not work that way."

It hissed and reached out to strike Morgain across the face. "I told you once, I have everyone in the end. The girl, you, all who desire to see their enemies struck down; they are all given to me, to grant their wish."

The sorceress stepped away, regal once more, and raised her chin, staring into the hooded shadows as though she could see what lay beneath, and banish it by sheer force of will.

Suddenly sidelined, Ailis's mind was racing even as she stood very still and hoped not to be noticed again. Morgain had used them. But, as Ailis had said to Gerard and Newt, everyone used them. Everyone had their own reason for doing things, saying things.

Evil is all in how you look at things.

Morgain had said that; it had been one of her first lessons to a much more idealistic Ailis.

The companion had used Morgain: used her ego, and her jealousy, and her love for the land she claimed the right to rule. Used that love, and twisted it to its own ends.

But what could they do with it? How could they use that note, that hint in Morgain's voice, before it was too late? Ailis's magic was weakened by her efforts with the rockslide. She was useless now.

Where was Newt? Gerard wondered.

There was a blur of action, and the sound of a high-pitched scream.

While the companion was distracted by Morgain's wavering commitment, Newt had gotten closer, unseen or ignored by everyone else. With one lunge, he had reached out and, in a diving move, grabbed at whatever lay underneath the figure's hood, and *pulled.*

The shadow-figure screamed.

Falling and rolling away, Newt looked down and saw a thin gray fabric in his hand, slippery and sheer, like a veil, only with a warm and unpleasant texture. He dropped it, disgusted, and rubbed his hand hard against the leg of his pants, trying to erase the memory of the touch, even as he got to his feet to defend himself against any counterattack.

What he saw was more terrible than any weapon. The hood had fallen back off a hairless skull, and the face glaring out at him was not human.

Shaped like a human's face, yes: a chin, mouth, nose, two eyes. But beyond that, it had as much in common with the dragon, or his salamander, as any of them. There was no skin on the flesh that held the features together, only a raw, oozing substance, white like the belly of a snake that had never seen sunlight. Raw like hunger.

And the eyes, the deep-set pits, which caused even Morgain to back down, were flame red; they were, in fact, flames, flickering inside that unholy skull with the heat of a hundred generations of impassioned prayers.

"Goddess, mother of us all," Morgain whispered, as taken aback by the revelation as anyone.

"What *is* it?" Gerard asked. "What have you called down upon us, Morgain?"

"Hatred. Hope. Fear. Anger. All the things soldiers left behind, when they returned to Mother Rome to save their own land, abandoning us as callously as they had arrived." Morgain swallowed tightly. "They broke my people, broke the Queen, brought their own gods, their own laws, all the things Arthur embraced. It seemed only right to use their own remnants, their own gods against him. . . ."

Something stirred in Newt's memory: some faded scrap of song or story, his mother's voice crooning to him, and he blurted out a name.

"Nemesis."

THIRTEEN

The name rang out in the grove like the sounding of a horn. It was filled with bloodlust, and with it came the knowledge to all of them of what they faced.

Nemesis: the Roman goddess of vengeance.

"She's supposed to have wings," Ailis said, reeling under the information flooding into her head. "Isn't she?"

"She?" Gerard was having trouble with that.

"Nemesis. The bringer of balance, punishing those who were too fortunate for no cause, those who do evil." Morgain smiled, a brittle smile that showed too many perfect teeth. "I summoned no small demon."

"You called a god!" Gerard was shaking, aware that his sword, his muscles, were all useless, but he was overwhelmed with the desire to do *something*.

Rage overwhelmed him. "You raised a god, made of the emotions of soldiers who hated us!" One of the many lessons crammed down the throats of all squires was that of the Romans who had come to Britain, and while the view in Camelot was different from Morgain's opinion of Rome's legacy, one thing that Gerard knew was that the Romans thought the natives to be little more than savages to be tamed, controlled, and absorbed into the might of their empire. Nemesis would have no desire to return Morgain's vision of Britain to reality—she would rather destroy it all.

The goddess in question raised one gloved hand, palm open as though to strike, and a blast of power sent Ailis staggering back, bloody scrapes appearing across her cheek.

"My name will not save you now, no matter what you might once have become. You will die, and the bargain will be sealed," Nemesis told her, advancing slowly toward the girl. "Balance will be restored. Chaos will return. This land will fall back to that as it was, as it was wished."

"That was not my wish!" Morgain protested. "I wanted peace, not—"

"Your intent does not matter," Nemesis said.

"Only your wish. Only that which was in your mind as you called me. Hatred. Disorder. Justice." She paused. "Revenge." The last word was spoken with such loving tones, all four humans shivered in response.

"My name will not save *you* now, either, Priestess," the shadow-figure crooned. "The bargain has been made. Revenge has a cost. All things have a cost. And it is time to pay."

Nemesis moved again toward Ailis, only to find her way blocked by Newt and Gerard, the latter forcing his leg to hold him upright while he raised his battered, dirt- and blood-covered sword in an act of useless defiance.

Off to the side, Morgain lifted her hands and began to speak in a low voice. Ailis, still on the ground, listened for a few beats, then began speaking as well, her words not so much matching the sorceress's as twining around them, adding to them.

"Begone, mortals!" Nemesis spat at the boys. Another wave of power knocked Gerard square in the knees, making him crumple to the ground, clutching at his leg. The stained and wrinkled bandage showed new blossoms of red underneath; the wound had reopened with the blow.

Newt felt the blow, and braced for it—only to feel it instead part and flow around him, like water around a stone.

His astonishment was matched only by Nemesis's. The goddess stared the boy in the face, eyes flaring even brighter as she raised her hand for another blow, then checked herself.

"What's the matter, can't do it?" Newt taunted the figure with a sense of tempting fate. A musical hum sounded in his ears, in the layers of bone beneath, under skin, under blood, but he had no time to wonder about it, no strength to listen to it.

Out of the corner of his eye, he saw Gerard, still crumpled and pale, rocking in pain, and Ailis, her eyes scrunched closed, trying to call enough magic to defeat a god. His friends were injured; his friends, who would die, far from home, without the glory that was rightfully theirs.

The hum tried to grow, but was pressed down by another noise; the serpentine sound of Nemesis's voice, hissing unfamiliar words Newt could almost make out. A spell, or some magic was trying to freeze his bones, shatter his will.

Something stirred deep inside himself, in an area he had never even noticed before. Something large, and hot, and ugly, the brute cousin of what he had felt when Merlin tried to enforce his will over them earlier. "Come on, knock me over! You're so powerful, so scary—do it!"

Unnoticed by any of the two-legged figures, the salamander crawled around in the banked fire, the activity stirring the coals back to life.

Nemesis snarled, but no further attack came, neither verbal nor physical. Clearly, the avatar wanted to strike Newt down, the same as the others . . . but something prevented it.

Newt grinned at it, the way a dog grins at prey just before it strikes.

"You hate this land so much? Drawing on all the frustration, the anger, whatever, of all those soldiers who called on you? Fine. Feed off that. But there's something you didn't think about, in your plan.

"My da's father was one of your damned soldiers. He raised my da to be a proper Roman boy, only it didn't work out that way. He wed a local girl, got her with a local-born son. And I'm not the only one, I bet, descended from your soldiers and living off the land you're so intent on wiping out."

Newt didn't know where all this knowledge was coming from; it was as though, with the information about Nemesis, other things, other memories had been shaken loose. His father had died when he was very young, but his mother had told him stories and sung him Roman songs. She had passed along an awareness, faint and forgotten though it had been, of all the blood that ran in his veins.

Blood that ran hot and fierce now; a soldier's blood, a warrior's blood. He had to fight, rend, *protect*.

"Go on, strike me!"

The next blow rebounded off Newt's chest and struck back at Nemesis. Newt swayed, but stayed on his feet, a barrier between Nemesis and Ailis. The girl was still trying to find some chink in the avatar's magical armor.

The goddess had come here through Morgain's invitation. But the basis of her strength was the blood of the soldiers who had invoked her name, generations before. Newt carried the blood of both within him, native and invader. Nemesis might strike at him, but not destroy; not without breaking the forces which allowed her access to this land, this land's magic, in the first place.

"If you're going to do something," Newt said, panting, to Ailis, "do it now."

Near the well, Gerard had rolled onto his side and fought through the pain in order to stand up.

"Ger . . . get away from here." Gerard was the one with the Grail. If Newt could keep Ailis safe, and Gerard could somehow get the Grail to Arthur . . .

As though sensing the direction of Newt's thoughts, Nemesis paused, then, with a snarl, leapt not at Newt, but Gerard, even as the squire tried to get to his feet to get away.

"No!" Ailis called, the sight breaking her concentration.

Newt's blood heated to boiling. *Destroy the threat.* Words flowed from him, harsh, ragged-edged words that none of them, not even Newt, recognized, and his arm drew back as though to throw something.

A long beam of light, shaped like a spear topped with a dark red point, appeared in his grasp.

He repeated the phrase, his voice getting louder, and let the spear fly.

It never left his hand—it *was* his hand, the light coming from it somehow fused with him—but a bolt went through the air, into Nemesis's shoulder, nonetheless.

Newt chanted another phrase and raised his left hand. In it, a straight, double-edged blade of light appeared. A gladius, a stabbing sword used by warriors in Newt's grandfather's day.

Newt's face twisted into something fierce, almost inhuman, and he rushed at Nemesis, the magical gladius held low and flat, aimed directly for the avatar's ribs.

The two met in a burst of black light; Nemesis tinged in purple, Newt in red—the color of dried blood.

Somewhere inside Newt, under the rage, a soft chime sounded again, and was swept away.

Morgain made her way to Ailis's side, having given up on her attempts to attack the companion. "It consumes him," the sorceress said, watching Newt. "Whatever magic he's using, it eats him alive from inside."

"Newt . . . has no magic," Ailis protested. And yet, it was impossible to deny. It was not a magic as she knew inside herself, the gentle flowing of tides, or the forms Morgain showed her, the brutal powers of earth and blood; it was not even the air-magics Merlin rode.

"Berserks," Morgain said. "Madman of the North. It will turn him into a beast. He will not be able to keep going as he is. We must be ready . . .

when his own magic destroys him, that will be our chance. Strike at Nemesis and free me. Free us all."

Ailis started to snap at Morgain—she was not willing to accept Newt's death—when a crackling noise behind her caught her attention. Constans was happily writhing in the coals, the heat making its skin glow with a dark, red-tinged light. Exactly like Newt's.

"It feeds off his heat," Morgain said, following her glance. "When he dies, it will freeze to death, no doubt. Useless . . ."

The two fighters shifted stances, Newt's blade trying another angle, Nemesis blocking it. Newt snarled, an animal sound rising from deep inside his chest. His flame darkened, the red tinge turning brighter, the band of it growing wider, inching toward his body.

"Not long now."

"No!" Ailis's cry was one of despair, cutting through the loud buzzing in Newt's ears, resonating in his blood, fueling his strength, his ability to fight, to defend, to defeat, and to rend his enemy. Some small part still aware inside him heard it, recognized it: Ailis, in pain.

There is a cost, a voice whispered to him, speaking

in tune with the small music still trying to hum in his bones.

You are glorious, another voice said. *Glorious and powerful and unstoppable.*

You will die, the first voice said.

All men die. Die in battle, as is your birthright!

Magic will kill you, my son. His mother's voice, the faintest whisper, long-buried in his memory but never forgotten. *Magic is not your destiny. Walk away from it. Refuse it. Live free of it.*

There is a cost to magic—Morgain's ties to the land, Merlin's backward-aging and absentmindedness, and Ailis's isolation. His price would be his life.

He didn't want to die.

Then live, the soft hum said inside him.

The rage snapped at him, like a dog straining at the leash, a horse pulling against the rein. Like the dogs he had trained, Newt gentled the snapping hound, overwhelming it, forcing it down into a lower position within the pack, forcing it to accept him as pack-leader.

Inch by inch, muscle by muscle, Newt tamed the beast inside him, forced it back into the space it had slept in all his life, slammed a door shut, and slid the bolt home.

Well done, the Grail hummed to him, pleased.

And with a brutal back-swipe, Nemesis sent him flying across the grove, landing with a thud against the well. The red faded entirely to black and disappeared.

FOURTEEN

"Fools. Mortal barbarian fools." Nemesis stood before Morgain, having discarded the hooded robe she had worn for so long. Terrible and awe-inspiring, beautiful and horrible; even if you did not believe in the old gods, the goddess was an impressive figure, from the hairless head and fire-lit eyes, all the way down to her clawed feet and back up to the massive wings, which even now flexed and flared behind her; white feathers tipped with purple.

"Did you think you could cheat Fate? Cheat me?" Nemesis's rage was focused on Morgain, who had tried to play both sides against each other, clearly planning to take on whoever had won while they were still weakened from the battle.

The sorceress reacted to this renewed threat the only way she knew how—with arrogance and pride.

Climbing to her feet, the sorceress faced down Nemesis. No more pretense, no more civility or shades of alliance. They were just two fierce and selfish powers, battling for dominance over each other.

Gerard saw all this through doubled vision. He had lost too much blood, first trying to keep up with Newt and Ailis, then in the battle with Nemesis. None of that was going to matter now. It was all over. They had been tricked. No matter what Morgain might want or not want, even now that Nemesis's control over her was broken, there seemed to be no way to stop the trap from closing around Camelot, perhaps destroying Arthur's reign forever.

"There's one way."

The voice was familiar, but Gerard had never heard it before. Like the knowledge of Nemesis, it seemed to come from deep within, planted there by some force. Unlike that knowledge, this had a distinct voice. A soft, deep, chime of a sound, that spoke not in words but tones of color, streaks of light, and peals of sound.

"One way to save all. Save from darkness."

Gerard looked around, blinked hard, forcing his eyes to focus. Across the way, past the two magical figures engaged in a contest of wills, he saw Ailis, looking as bewildered as he felt.

"Let me go. Let the waters wash the sin, cleanse the soil, free the soul."

"The Grail." Ailis's lips barely moved, and there was no way he could hear her across the distance, but she could have shouted for the impact it made. Instinctively, Gerard's hand clenched on the bag, making sure that the cup was still within.

His first instinct was to deny the words, deny the voice. This was the meaning of the Quest, the key to his future. With it, Arthur's rule was assured, fame and glory achieved, his name written into history now and forever. Without it, he was a squire whose greatest stories would be buried for the sake of Arthur's rule and Merlin's reputation. He would be valued, yes, but never famous. Never one of the knights remembered through the generations.

He could not do what the voice was suggesting. He couldn't.

Then Newt stirred, but just barely. Ailis reached out a hand to reassure him, to warn him against moving too much and attracting Nemesis's attention again. Newt stilled, then rolled over slowly onto his side, taking in the scene at a glance. The two boys' gazes met, and Gerard was struck by the despair, the loss, he saw in Newt's eyes.

"I tried," Newt said. "I tried, and failed. I could not use my rage to destroy her."

Rage and sorrow filled Gerard, then. A knight was not someone who sought fame. A true knight was one who protected the innocent, the weak; who did what was needful because it was needful, no matter the cost.

He, Gerard, was still a squire. He might always remain a squire. But he knew one truth that had nothing to do with sitting at the Round Table: There was more to being a knight than honor or fame. There was friendship, loyalty, and love.

And no one should ever be allowed to look the way Newt looked just then, as though he had given everything, won every battle . . . only to lose the war. No one who had triumphed over hatred, the way Newt had, should ever think that he had failed.

Every inch of his body protested, but Gerard unclenched his hand, reached into the leather bag, and withdrew the Grail. It shimmered once in his hold, the echoes of that chiming voice stroking the inside of his ears, then sound and shimmer both subsided, as though something had hushed it.

Newt could hear it, and Ailis. Gerard could tell

from the way they looked at it.

Just a cup. Just a simple, wooden cup, stained and cracked. Nothing worthy of note.

Gerard rose to his feet, feeling his leg wobble underneath him. Moving slowly, cautiously, he staggered to the well. Newt, lying on the grass where he had fallen, looked from the Grail to Gerard as he came closer and nodded, once. "Yes," his lips moved, although no sound came from them.

As though watching someone else's hand, Gerard lifted the Grail over the turquoise waters.

"No!" The shadow figure had finally noticed what Gerard was doing. She turned away from Morgain to try and stop him.

And then Newt was impossibly up on his feet, tackling Nemesis; not in a berserker rage, but as a mere mortal soul. His mixed-breed blood, the blood of two lands, was just enough to cause Nemesis to hesitate long enough for Gerard to open his fingers, and watch the cup fall, turning slowly, into the bitter blue waters.

"Nemesis!" Ailis called, her voice scratched and hoarse, but triumphant. "Leave! Be gone from these lands!"

The cup seemed to fall forever, but all too soon a

splash rose up, hitting the walls of the well, washing away the soot-drawn symbols and leaving the stones clean.

Morgain screamed once in denial, but the goddess's scream was shriller, high-pitched and piercing, like the howl of the bansidhe, the fairy creature who foretells death.

Ailis ran to Newt, pulled him upright, and checked to make sure he was all right.

Gerard's heart clenched in pain—after all he had given up, he saw that she went to the stable boy first. Then her hand reached out for his, and he clasped her fingers and let himself be drawn into a three-way hug.

The scream built and built, a hot wind rising around them, powerful thunder crashing inside the cavern until all three had no choice but to cover their ears and huddle together until it stopped.

When they finally uncurled themselves from the ground, everything was gone. Morgain, Nemesis, the well. The ground was scored clean, the grass gone. The nearest trees were uprooted and slanting against each other.

"The Grail?" It wasn't really a question, but Gerard answered Newt anyway.

"Gone."

Ailis blinked grit and tears from her eyes, and looked over her shoulder. "Constans! He's gone, too."

In fact, the entire fire pit was gone, and with it, the salamander.

"I think . . . I think facing what I was . . . what I could be, and then rejecting it. I think I sent it away," Newt said sadly.

"Because it was magic?"

"Because it was me. In a way. That's why I named it what I did, I guess."

"Constans. That's a Roman name. Like your grand-da."

"Like me," Newt corrected her. "Constans is the name my folks gave me. But my ma always called me Newt. Little Newt."

"Because your magic was tied to fire."

Newt shrugged. "Maybe. I'll never know."

"So who are you?" Gerard asked.

"I'm me," Newt said, after a long pause. "Morgain was wrong. True names are power, but the name your parents give you isn't always the true name."

"But the magic . . ."

"Gone." He was lying—Newt could feel the

magic still simmering, locked away down inside him. But he had no intention of ever calling on it again. Unlike Ailis, he felt no pangs of loss. It wasn't fun, wasn't part of him he liked, but a killing tool, one he had no desire to wield. He was a stable boy, not a soldier.

"Not all magic is bad," Ailis said, with the tone of someone who had argued the point one time too many.

"No," Newt agreed, his arm around her shoulders. Not when you choose it, rather than being overrun by it. Ailis had learned that when she walked away from Morgain and the sorceress's lures. She went back, yes, but under her own terms, her own choice. She walked into that fire with a goal, and never lost sight of it. Just as he chose not to use his. It was his inheritance. But it wasn't his life.

Gerard looked around the cavern again, at the trees, the cave walls, and his two bedraggled and battered friends, then flopped onto his back with a heavy sigh.

"Nobody," he said with a sigh, "is going to believe this."

"Merlin will," Newt said. "Or maybe he already knows and forgot. Or something like that. Merlin makes my head hurt."

The three friends smiled at each other in weary accord.

* * *

Some time later, the three of them staggered out of the melted hole in the cavern's entrance, blinking at the dawn sunlight filling the sky.

"How long were we in there?" Newt wondered.

"No idea," Gerard said. "It felt like . . ."

"Forever," Ailis said. "Forever and a day, and an entire life."

"I'm hungry." Newt's comment was so matter-of-fact, it sent them all into fits of laughter. "Well, I am," he protested. "Like I'm all hollow inside. You aren't?"

"I am, actually," Ailis said thoughtfully. "Maybe all the magic we were using . . ."

"Or maybe we just haven't eaten all day. Days. However long it really has been. I'd eat the dragon, if he didn't have all those scales," Gerard said.

"And if taking a bite wouldn't maybe wake him up again?" Ailis said.

"More to the point, anyone have any idea how we're getting home?" Newt asked. His arm was still around Ailis; a combination of bone-weariness and Newt's own relaxation made it seem like the most natural thing in the world. "Seeing as how Ailis has run dry, magically, Sir Tawny's long gone, and we haven't a horse or coin to our names?"

"We walk," Ailis said, ever practical. "At least until I can reach out and contact Merlin again."

"Great. We're dependent on a sorcerer who flies into walls to rescue us. I'm so confident, now." Magical or not, Newt was still Newt.

"It's going to be a very, very long trip." Gerard sighed as he adjusted his pack on his back and started down the hill. "A very, very long trip . . ."

EPILOGUE

"And so the Grail was won . . . and lost again. How *is* my dear brother taking that bit of news?"

Morgain called a chair up out of nothingness and seated herself in it, her fur-trimmed gown flowing around her in graceful folds. The chair was a dark wood, ornate but not massive, and it suited her perfectly.

Merlin leaned against an invisible wall, watching her with ironic amusement.

She was selfish, and single-minded, and dedicated to a way of life that would not come again. And she had focused her entire adult life to destroying the things he had spent his entire life building and protecting: Arthur, Camelot, the future. Yet he respected her greatly, feared her a little, and would never, ever, let her know either.

"Quite well, actually," he said, answering her question. "The powers of darkness were not able to take it away from us, after all—the virtue of his knights and their companions was enough to hold them at bay, and save the land from darkness and despair once again. The minstrels have been singing of nothing else all month. Or is it next month? Or last month? I'm about to go mad from the noise, either way."

"You were already mad, Merlin," Morgain said dryly.

For Merlin, madness was the only way to stay sane and do what he needed to do. It had been too close, this game. Far too close, from start to finish. He had won this round.

His pawns—Ailis, Gerard, and Newt—had played their roles perfectly. They had even managed to surprise him: Who knew that the lowly stable boy held so much power within him? The temptation to pry, to pull the berserker energy out of the boy and harness it somehow was almost overwhelming. But he would not do that. Not only would it be wrong, but Ailis would never speak to him again. And he would rather have one willing protégé than two unwilling ones.

It was one more than Morgain had.

"She will not be yours, you know." Morgain had the not-surprising ability to read him like a book, here in the astral plane.

His skills with women were as bad here as they were on earth. But that did not mean he was totally without a clue.

"She will be her own," he said calmly, calling in a goblet filled with sweet well-water. With a tinge of maliciousness, he made the goblet clear, like ice, and then colored the water the exact shade of turquoise blue of the Aegean, the color of Nemesis's home shores. "Her own, and her faithful Roman's, that is."

Morgain made a face. She had nothing against the stable boy—she had nothing against anyone with magic so deep in their bones. But his Roman blood had cost her greatly, and she resented that. As Merlin knew she did.

"She will be her own," Merlin repeated. "When you and I are gone, and Arthur has fallen, as we both know he eventually will, Ailis and Constans's children will continue."

"Children?" She raised an eyebrow at that. "Assuming a bit, are you not? Or have you seen the actual birthing?" His ability to live backward could be useful, if you could pry through the nonsensical patter that so often accompanied one of his bouts of confusion.

"Call it a hunch," he said. "They will have children of magic, on both sides. Children of magic to hold the land; to speak to it and appease it. We rise and fall, and the bloodlines change, but the land adapts. It always has. Your kind were not the first, Morgain. Other blood has nourished the soil over the generations, and will do so again. Even Romans. They loved this land, too. They did not all leave willingly when their empire ordered them to return."

The sorceress clearly did not agree, but chose not to follow up on that point, staring at her opponent for a moment.

"Will they love the land enough, Merlin?" she finally asked. She was not looking for reassurance, but rather asking as one great general to another, conferring on the status of armies marshaling in the field.

"If they don't, it will be their failure, not ours," was all he could say. "Good night, Morgain. Do not try to harm them again."

She laughed then, a sweet, clear, evil laugh. "You

do not command me, Merlin. I will harm them or not, as I choose."

He bowed to her, mockingly, and faded from view, his hawk-sharp eyes watching her until every other feature of his body had disappeared. Then he blinked, and was entirely gone.

"As I choose," Morgain repeated, relishing the sound of the words, and then she, too, departed the astral plane, fading into wisps of dark golden light.

*   *   *

Safe and secure in the great stone in the Orkneys, Morgain's physical body slowly stretched, waking out of a deep sleep. Still drained from the effort of defeating Nemesis and protecting her chosen successor, she barely had the strength to raise the waiting cup of hot chocolate to her lips. Her body might be weak still, but her mind was finally clear of Nemesis's malevolent influences. She was her own woman once more and had no desire to hand over any sort of control ever again—no matter what anyone might promise her, no matter how tempting.

Merlin had won this round. But there were endless turns of the day yet to come. And, despite Merlin's pretty words, she was not willing to leave her legacy to chance.

Ailis and the stable boy would marry and have children. No doubt Merlin was counting on their love of the loyal and noble squire, Gerard, to keep them tied to his precious Camelot. And it would likely be so.

But even loyal knights could be subverted, if you offered them the right bait. Perhaps she would leave Ailis and her friends be, to see what they might, in fact, grow up to become. If Merlin was correct, as well as mad, Ailis might yet become a powerful ally, and her menfolk along with her.

Morgain thought it best to focus on other links in the chain surrounding Arthur's throne first. The great and noble Lancelot was a good place to start. Incorruptible Sir Lancelot. Finding *his* weakness would be interesting.

The great cat slept at the foot of her bed, stretched full-length, ears twitching in dreams of chasing giant mice.

With a contented sigh, Morgain went back to sleep, willing her body to heal, and smiling about the plots yet to come. The battle for the Old Ways was far from over, and she'd have many more chances to take action.

And, in the window of her bed chamber, a small owl clucked mournfully, then spread its sawdust-stuffed wings, and flew away.